Poppy and Mary Ellen Deliver the Goods

MISSION POINT PRESS

Published by Mission Point Press
2554 Chandler Rd.
Traverse City, MI 49696
(231) 421-9513
www.MissionPointPress.com

ISBN: 978-1-958363-70-6
Library of Congress Control Number: 2023903114
Printed in the United States of America

Poppy and Mary Ellen Deliver the Goods

Book One
of the Frankenmuth Murder Mysteries

For Martin Tyckoski

(1945 – 2021)

who would have laughed in all the right places
and asked all the right questions.

Love you.
—Roz

CONTENTS

1: MARY ELLEN AND POPPY: PRIVATE EYES

Mary Ellen Freeman drove her little silver-blue convertible down Main Street in Frankenmuth on her way to meet her friend at the Harvest Coffee Shop. The city's German heritage was evident in the architecture of the buildings and in shopkeepers' dress. Dirndls and lederhosen were commonly seen around town. Mary Ellen always appreciated this little city, where she had lived with her husband, Todd, for twenty-some years.

The Harvest had two levels. Mary Ellen spotted her good friend Poppy Lutz in one of the comfortable chairs.

"Do you need a coffee?" asked Mary Ellen.

"All set. I saved you a seat," replied Poppy.

Poppy and Mary Ellen had met years ago at the library. Mary Ellen was the former librarian and current mah-jongg maven of Frankenmuth. Poppy was an avid reader and mah-jongg player who had been a private investigator. They had bonded over a love of mysteries, and lately had made it their literal business as investigative partners.

"So, let's divide up the jobs for today," Poppy suggested when Mary Ellen sat down with her coffee.

"Well, you take the dogs (as always) and I'll take the Wilson husband and see if I can document any hanky-panky going on there with the dental hygienist."

"Great. You know I'd rather chase dogs anytime," said Poppy, "and I have three on the loose around town. I'll check with all three owners in case their dogs showed up."

Poppy and her husband had moved to Frankenmuth a few years before the Freemans. David, Poppy's late husband, had been an attorney of some note. He was sorely missed by his clients and the community and greatly missed by Poppy. They had had many dogs over the years, the most famous being Jethro, their dog who loved being part of the library's popular reading program.

Jethro had gone over the Rainbow Bridge several years ago. Poppy, who hated being in the house alone, had rescued another Boston terrier, Babycakes. But Babycakes, who was a great companion, was not ever going to be a library dog. She found too many things alarming and was a "see something, say something" kind of dog.

Poppy's dogs were as individualistic as Poppy herself. After years of hating her thinning hair, she had purchased several wigs of different colors and styles. Today's was an ash-blonde number with wispy bangs. She never worried about consistency with her wigs. Mary Ellen was a tall woman with short, white hair held back by a headband which matched her shirt and shoe colors. Her shoes were often bright Crocs. She always looked well put together.

They had just finished their planning when the coffee house door slammed open. There stood Clare the caterer. She spotted Mary Ellen and Poppy.

"I need your help. My van broke down and is being towed, but I have a load of food to take up to the Residenz Inn. Can you help? Please?"

Mary Ellen and Poppy knew Clare only slightly, but were willing to make a quick trip to help her out. Or at least Mary Ellen, always the more gracious of the two, was. Poppy leaned over and whispered, "Look, I have dogs to round up. I don't want to get caught up in someone's catering job."

Mary Ellen kept smiling and whispered back, "Don't be that way. She just wants a little delivery help."

"Great," muttered Poppy to herself, thinking that all the missing dogs might be sitting on their own front porches without her assistance any time now.

When they got outside, the tow truck was hooking up a white van. "Wait a second," Clare said to the tow-truck driver. "We need to transfer some things from the van. Which car is yours?" Mary Ellen pointed to the small convertible, and Poppy pointed to her large, white minivan.

Clare looked relieved at the larger vehicle. That is, until she looked in the back. The minivan was packed with all kinds of stuff—leashes, water dishes and bottles of water, a small dog crate, Milk Bones here and there, poop bags, barf towels, a couple squeaky toys, a tennis ball, and more. Mary Ellen stifled a giggle and helped move everything as far forward as possible. They got all the containers transferred and drove to the Residenz.

2: LIKE A HORSE AND CARRIAGE

Twenty-eight-year-old Mark had been a driver for the Heritage Carriage Tour Company for very nearly ten years, long enough to do what no high school English class could manage—create in him a sense of irony. While he was always in forward motion with the horse, his life wasn't going anywhere. But ten years was a long time. Depending on his probable lifespan (which someone at the Frankenmuth Insurance Company could certainly tell him), it could be fourteen percent or more of his entire existence. But it was a long time to spend your days looking at the back end of, in his case, the only spotted pony who was part of the Carriage Tour stables.

The pony was always two steps ahead of Mark, who had ample time to stare at those spots from the vantage point of his carriage seat. The spots were becoming one of those inkblot tests.

That afternoon, he had a private tour scheduled for a single old lady as his passenger. It would be the first time he picked anyone up at the recently renovated Residenz, an impressive, columned home recently added to the lodging choices in Frankenmuth. It was cold and pouring rain, but apparently the old lady was a trouper. With a little luck, he'd be tipped well, make a little extra on the side, and end the day with pizza and beer at Tiffany's Food and Spirits. He showed up ten minutes early to pick up his passenger.

•••

Virginia Stanley walked out of the Residenz accompanied by her nephew, Ned. She was the only member of the Stanley family reunion who had chosen to take a carriage ride. A lot of togetherness lay ahead. Ned and the array of cousins and significant others had gathered, armed with videos, photo albums, and memories. That being said, they mostly were gathering to get a feel for where all the Stanley money would go when Aunt Virginia, keeper of the family fortune, was gone, and perhaps have a last-ditch chance to influence things.

The carriage, decorated for autumn, pulled in, the driver wearing a top hat and fall-colored striped scarf.

"Hello, Mrs. Stanley. I'm Mark, and will be showing you the sites around town this afternoon."

"Terrific, Mark. I'm happy to have some time to myself away from the rest of the family to relax and look around. But I guess I have to get back in time for dinner with everyone."

"Ned told me all about the 5:00 p.m. time. No problem!"

Virginia leaned back and relaxed while Mark leaned down to tell her about the passing places of interest. "You do an impressive job of driving and talking to whoever is behind you in the carriage," she complimented him. "But don't feel you need to give too much detail. I'm just looking forward to a pleasant ride and a break from the next generation waiting for me to die."

Mark had nothing to say to that, which made for a quieter ride. As they pulled onto Main Street, Virginia reached into her purse and pulled out her grandfather's silver flask. A few nips of gin would make the Gather and Graze a much smoother evening.

Frankenmuth was a meticulously maintained town and always seasonally decorated. The town was particularly known for flowers—coordinated by the florist in town with the color combinations of the year—both planted and hung up and down blocks of Main Street. The decorations, plants, and flowers were funded by local businesses as well as ordinary citizens who simply gave money out of civic pride. Seasonal distinctions for fall always included corn stalk arrangements. Tourists were normally taken with the decorations.

Virginia, however, was more preoccupied with her impending estate planning disclosure and not really attentive to the flowers. A nip every time the carriage stopped seemed a good way to pace her afternoon sips.

They had an abrupt moment when a big white-and-black dog ran right in front of the horse on his way across the street, seemingly on a mission. Mark muttered an expletive to himself and said to Virginia, "Sorry about that. It's a local dog, Munchie. What a hazard."

Three nips later, the carriage came to a lengthy stop. Virginia looked out the door and saw that a van was being hooked up to a tow truck and the process had stalled traffic.

It seemed that the tow truck couldn't move because there were three women unloading the van's cargo and putting it into another vehicle. Since they were stopped, Virginia took another sip. The carriage took a turn and started up the hill into a residential area. She closed her eyes just for a moment.

3: ON THE SCENE

Back at the Residenz, the family had settled in. In addition to Virginia, her nephew, Joe (son of her sister, Dakota), and his wife, Amelia, there were the twins, Nelly and Nora (daughters of her sister, Carolina), and their brother, Ned, with his fiancé, Arrabella. They were all to meet in the Great Room at five o'clock for the kickoff event of the weekend. The invitation from Aunt Gin (her love of her flask and gin was a family legend) was a bit of a surprise. While no one was looking forward to the weekend, no one would dare miss it.

Joe made a general announcement before they all scattered. "Everyone, please be downstairs, ready to welcome Virginia at five o'clock when her carriage ride ends. Let's all do our best to look sharp and as though we are loving being here together. And for God's sake, remember to say Aunt Virginia ... not Aunt Gin." Absolutely everyone was muttering to whomever they were closest at being given deportment instructions from Joe.

●●●

At five o'clock sharp, Mark steered the carriage into the circular driveway. The family had been joined by the high-profile innkeeper and owner, Judy, dressed in a business Bavarian outfit, on the front veranda. It marked her as a boss. She told friends that her Bavarian garb was the equivalent of a man's suit.

Mark jumped down and reached into the carriage to help Virginia out to be greeted by her family. Mark looked puzzled, then bent all the way in. He stepped back and literally screamed in shock. Joe pushed forward and got into the carriage. He yelled, "Aunt Virginia! Aunt Virginia?" He jumped out and turned to the people in front of him. "I think ... it looks like ... Aunt Virginia is dead." His wife, Amelia, a nurse, leaned into the carriage. She reappeared, blood on her hands, and confirmed what Joe had guessed. Judy had already called 911, and her next call was to her own head of security.

●●●

Every cruiser in town—more than one might imagine in a city of five thousand residents—rolled over the scenic covered bridge with lights flashing but no sirens. On the chance everyone was still alive but in need of help, the fire department also responded. A paramedic hopped off the fire truck with a medical bag in hand and raced over to the carriage. Judy and the chief of police, Ed, exchanged glances and Judy gave a slight shrug.

The paramedic established there was nothing the fire department could do for Virginia, and backed off while Ed took in the buggy scene and the body. In his years in Frankenmuth, he had seen a buggy accident or two but had never seen anyone die on a tour in one of the carriages. "This isn't good," he said.

Ed called a contact in the nearby Michigan State Police Crime Unit, telling him they could use help processing this scene right away. Other police officers, as well as Judy's security people, pushed curious tourists back with the suggestion that they might want to go have a beer.

Poppy and Mary Ellen were right there when the carriage showed up, having finished helping Clare deliver food. Indeed, they always somehow seemed to show up at anything odd.

The duo had stumbled on interesting situations in their amateur detective activities that had been useful to law enforcement. As Ed looked around at the queue of relatives, it appeared that this was a complicated family. He would get to them, but he talked to Mark first. "We can't let you return the horse and carriage, Mark. The carriage is a crime scene, and we don't even know for sure whether the horse might have some evidence on him. The Michigan Forensics Unit is arriving soon and will process the carriage. Meantime, are you the only witness on the scene, other than your horse, who may have witnessed the murder?"

"What? No! I didn't witness anything but the usual traffic, and I was talking to the old lady most of the time. I'm ready to go home!"

"Let me rephrase this for you, Mark. Your passenger got her throat cut and bled out in your carriage. You can't seem to explain this. Don't go anywhere. We are going to interview people at the Residenz—everyone in the family is staying there. And it's a good space. As I'm sure you are aware, we have a small police station. We might have follow-up questions for you after we talk to others. One consolation—I hear great food is waiting back there."

"My God. I have no idea what happened! I just want one other thing to be clear," said Mark. "I certainly have not ever seen the inside of your police station."

Judy sidled over to Mark and said, "Have you had a chance to see the renovations in the Residenz, Mark? There's a caterer in there who can fix you up with a sandwich and something to drink. Go on in and see what looks good." Classic innkeeper—feed them and let them calm down.

"I wouldn't mind seeing it, thanks. And I could use a sandwich." Two cops on the door took his name and basic contact information and let him in.

4: WHEN ONE NAME WON'T DO

Mary Ellen and Poppy rushed inside to the kitchen, anxious to scope out the family of the dead woman and share information. As they passed through the dining room, they noticed a bartender had set up the drinks cart. He was nice looking, and Poppy noticed he was somewhat older than most bartenders in town. The cart was set up precisely with all the bottles lined up by height, and the glasses organized by style. He looked up at the two ladies and nodded. They both slowed down and greeted him.

Mary Ellen breathlessly said, "Hi, we're with the caterer. I think there has been a change in plans for tonight. You might want to check with the police."

The bartender looked puzzled and repeated, "The police? I thought this was a family reunion."

Poppy grabbed Mary Ellen to move her forward. "We don't mean to be rude, but we have some kitchen things to do. The group should be along shortly." With that, the friends hustled off to the kitchen.

"Clare, you'll never guess—the lady who set this up is dead. She died on the carriage ride. The police, fire department, and Judy are all outside, and it seems likely that everyone is a suspect."

"Good heavens! The lady died? Do we still serve food? She died? Did she have a heart attack or something?"

Poppy and Mary Ellen grabbed full platters for the table. Even if this was going to turn into a police investigation, people still needed to eat. As they walked out of the kitchen they noticed the garage-like door over the counter. It was fitted with cut-glass inserts and separated the kitchen from the dining room.

"That will make serving and clearing so much easier. Let's raise it up," said Poppy, far more focused on information gathering than food serving.

"Perfect for serving and listening," said Mary Ellen. At the coffee house, they had perfected the art of eavesdropping. People tended to talk without lowering voices or checking their surroundings. As they moved platters from the kitchen to the dining room, the bartender was moving his drinks cart in the Great Room. People had begun to trickle in. Several headed right for the bartender.

Chief Ed and Judy were having a quiet discussion on the murder in Frankenmuth, a town so safe and friendly the chamber of commerce phone number was 1-800-FUN-TOWN, a true family destination. "We don't want to scare the wits out of the tourists, Ed," noted Judy. "There's no reason for others to be worried. Is there?"

"I think it's some kind of family thing, Judy. We'll keep it as low key as we can."

"Ladies and gentlemen. Please find a comfortable place to sit. My name is Chief Edward Swartz, of the Frankenmuth Police Department. My deputy and I will be taking preliminary statements tonight. I realize this is a shock and you'll want to spend time together as a family to grieve the loss of your aunt. When your aunt reserved the Residenz she said her family would be staying with her. Is everyone here?"

No one spoke. The chief looked at Joe and repeated, "Is everyone here?" Joe looked around the room and nodded.

As the chief got set up for questioning, Judy walked into the kitchen. "Ladies, thank you for staying. I could send more staff up, but it's late to move people around. You know what's going on out there. Would it be possible for you to stack dishes and come back in the morning to clear the rest out?" Poppy and Mary Ellen looked to Clare, but she had turned white and seemed on the verge of collapse.

Mary Ellen answered, "I'm sure we can make that work."

Judy nodded. "Thank you," she said, and quickly walked out the door.

Poppy turned to Clare. "Are you all right?"

Clare still looked pale. She tugged on her ruffled black apron, took off her baseball cap with CC (Clare's Catering) printed on it, and pushed her brown hair out of her eyes. She stared back at her friends. "No, I may be in some trouble here. Let's finish setting up, and I'll fill you in."

The three women quickly filled the rest of the dishes and set them on the table. "Grab a coffee and let me tell you my story."

Poppy looked at Mary Ellen and said, "Get the story from Clare. I'm going out to see what's happening with the police. You never know. We might be needed."

Clare and Mary Ellen settled in some comfy kitchen chairs. Clare cleared her throat. "I grew up in the same small town as Virginia Stanley. We all knew the Stanley family who ruled the town. After my parents died, I decided to start a catering company. I had taken a few culinary classes at the local community college and was ready to take the plunge. It was slow going, but eventually I started getting more and more business."

Mary Ellen interrupted, "Clare, so you are a caterer from Ohio? Why are you here?"

"First, my real name is Maris, and my big breakthrough turned into my waterloo. Virginia Stanley was in charge of the annual hospital fundraiser. She called me out of the blue to ask for estimates and menu options. I put together a very detailed proposal with table decor, food choices, and signature drink ideas. I also gave her an excellent price, hoping that this would make my name as the premier caterer in northwestern Ohio. She accepted all my ideas and price point.

"The event was spectacular. The weather was beautiful. The tables had white table cloths and small nosegays of colorful flowers. Charcuterie boards, petit fours, spring rolls, and mini crab quiches were included. I received so many compliments. I had made a name for myself. Until the next morning, when Virginia called to tell me many people had taken ill with food poisoning and my food was to blame.

"There was a stomach flu going around and I was sure that it was the culprit. But by then, Virginia had told everyone that my food was to blame. I had three cancellations and no new orders in the next three months. So, I came here to start over again. I really am going to need your help. These people know me, and I am going to be suspect number one.

"On top of losing my business, having to change my name, moving out of town and out of state, and trying to rebuild a financial future, I suffered a worse loss."

"What could top that?" asked Mary Ellen.

"My rescue dog, Cliff. I lost Cliff because of Virginia Stanley. I couldn't afford to keep him with me anymore, couldn't afford his allergy medicine, and had no idea if I could find a place to stay that would let Cliff in. He was my best friend, my companion, my heart. And I had to re-home him. Back he went to the rescue, which then found another permanent home for him, so there's no chance of getting him back.

"I have loved dogs all my life, and this terrible woman rips away the one creature who loved me unconditionally. And I let him down." Clare started sobbing.

Mary Ellen got up and hugged Clare/Maris. "Oh, I'm so sorry," she said. "Dogs are family. I know how that must hurt. But no matter how badly you were treated, you were right here at the time Mrs. Stanley was murdered. It's not like you could have done it for any reason. You were with us the entire time."

Mary Ellen grabbed a tray. "Poppy and I will circulate with food when she's done watching the police, maybe do a little listening, and report back. Clare, put your baseball cap back on, pull yourself together, and stay in the kitchen." Clare smiled to herself when Mary Ellen left the room.

5: MANNER OF DEATH IS...

Just like on TV, the Michigan Forensics Unit pulled up near the police presence. Chief Ed was explaining to Judy that processing the scene and examining the body are two different matters. "Services are slow right now, with autopsies and cases backed up. As a potential murder, this should get priority, but it's hard to say about the availability of someone with medical examiner experience."

Judy rolled her eyes skyward and said, "Geduld," her famous word for when patience was required. But she added, "We can't just wait around here." She picked up her cellphone yet again and called a friend, Doc Adams, who was a retired coroner for the county. She asked him if he could get this show on the road and off her property.

He was, he confirmed, still qualified to perform these services. Truth be told, he was very qualified by the standards of the moment pressing your average internist into reluctant duty. He showed up in five minutes.

Ed commented, "You got here fast. Thanks."

"Are you kidding me? The chance to help solve a murder in Frankenmuth? Priceless."

Between the doc and the techs, a quick preliminary investigation was made of Virginia's body. The doc told Ed, Judy, and Poppy, "Death appears to be caused by exactly what you said, Ed, exsanguination as a result of an injury to the left carotid artery, made by an unknown and missing sharp instrument wielded by an unknown person. Homicide."

Doc supervised the ambulance attendants who loaded Virginia on board and hustled her off quietly to the medical examiner's office in downtown Saginaw. He got inside his car, waved to Judy, and took off behind the ambulance.

Ed was muttering to one of his officers, "Damn it! Sure, it looks obvious. But how did that happen so quietly that that carriage driver didn't even know it and just kept yammering to her about the local brewery and coffee shop as they passed by? Are they telling me we could have buggies loaded with dead tourists and no one would even notice until the drivers stopped to unload the passengers? That just isn't possible. There's no way," he sputtered while his officers nodded in agreement. No one had died in a buggy up to now. And the story of how this happened made no sense. Mark was definitely not off the hook here. He was, in fact, suspect number one. But what on Earth could his motive be?

Suddenly, there was Poppy. Hadn't she gone back inside to the kitchen? She was standing among the police like a poodle in a circle of German shepherds. "Oh, Ed," she said, "I can see how upset you are, but you'll solve this in no time. It's not like bodies are going to start falling all over Frankenmuth."

"Don't you have dogs to find, Poppy? Are all the dogs suddenly home now and absolutely none of them needs you to scoop them up and give them a ride in your mutt-mobile? Don't you have little sandwiches to help with in the kitchen? And why can't you park your car straight?"

Ed stopped himself. He liked Poppy. She found his dog once. And he knew this case was already getting to him. Poppy sniffed at the rejection of her reassuring words. And she'd seen enough Acorn TV to know that bodies were certainly going to start falling all over Frankenmuth. This was, as they say, a cold whodunit.

Poppy retreated to the kitchen. She was in fact dressed for dog chasing—and had three clients who very much wanted their dogs home at the moment. She had only come out to offer Ed and the crime scene people some delicate little sandwiches. Well. That was what she told Mary Ellen and Clare, but it wasn't the only reason to be there. She really wanted to see what was going on at the scene. She wasn't sure she could return the sandwiches to the kitchen. "It's not like I'm some kind of expert on restaurant food law," she thought peevishly. She crammed a few sandwiches in her plastic-lined sweatshirt pocket, since sooner or later she needed to round up Roscoe, Chuckie, and Munchie. Meanwhile, the spotted pony called Ace was a calm and collected beast. Poppy figured he had had enough also and was right in the same camp as Chief Ed that this just was an unfathomable day.

•••

The crime scene techs were going to be there a while photographing every drop of blood and collecting samples, picking up every hair they could find, equine or human, and any debris. The techs could find no blood on Ace—not that that was completely simple to determine. He stood still for a fine-tooth combing, all hair collected, and enjoyed an apple from the carriage company's handler, who was there to collect both horse and buggy.

"You can take your horse now," the tech said to the carriage manager.

"What about my carriage?"

The tech commented, "It's going to be a while before you see the buggy again. We are putting it in a trailer and taking it over to the crime lab. It will have to be released by a bunch of people in the crime investigation chain, on up to the prosecutor's office, I'm guessing, before you can pick it up again."

He sighed and left with Ace, who had earned a drink of water and some decent feed. Maybe even a day off.

The chief instructed two officers to follow Ace's route that day to see if they could find anything of use. They also needed to establish, for all buildings on the route, who was present when Ace went by pulling his hearse.

He then turned his eye to the Residenz door, also sighed, and walked in.

6: TIME TO TALK TO THE FAMILY

As Chief Ed turned to go back into the house to question everyone, he saw Detective C.J. Bauer pull up. As soon as she had read the all-police text, she headed over to the Residenz.

"Well, what have we got here?" she asked. They had a murder—odd in Frankenmuth, and odder still at the Residenz.

Chief Ed filled her in on the basics, from the shocking murder to what was next. "Her family and the carriage driver are inside waiting to be questioned. Let's see if we can figure out where everyone was during the carriage ride time frame."

As they walked into the Great Room, they realized that the drinks cart had been popular. Almost everyone had a glass of something alcoholic, which could either work for or against them during questioning. People were sitting around the coffee table, with the exception of one man who was in the corner with a beer. The chatting stopped as soon as the pair of officers arrived.

"Ladies and gentlemen, I would like to introduce Detective C.J. Bauer. She will be assisting me with interviews. We'll be using the dining room as our temporary office."

He turned and spotted Poppy. "Poppy, would you and Mary Ellen serve food on trays so that no one has to come into the dining room unless they are with us?" Poppy nodded and went off to refill her tray and get Mary Ellen. The amateur detectives were fine helping out because it meant they were hanging out, too.

"Mark, I'd like to start with you. Follow me, please. And Detective Bauer will talk to…" he looked down at the list of family member guests, "Joe."

Mark and the chief went to the alcove in the dining room while C.J. and Joe sat at the table. Both put their phones on the tables to record conversations.

"Mark, how long have you been a driver for the Heritage Carriage Tour Company?" Ed asked.

"Ten years," said Mark.

Then he asked Mark to recall the day's events.

"I picked up the lady at the Residenz—something that was prearranged and out of the ordinary. One of the family members walked her out to the carriage. I hopped down to help her into the carriage, but she was pleasant enough. She told a nephew apparently that he and the rest of the family should be downstairs at precisely five o'clock. He said he wouldn't miss it for the world. I drove through town—the usual route—telling her about points of interest. She didn't respond or ask any questions at all. Then, I brought her back, right on time."

"Anything unusual along the way?"

"There was a traffic jam at Main and Cass—a broken-down van. I did happen to look back at one point and saw my passenger drinking out of a silver flask. That's about it."

"I'm going to need to talk to you again tomorrow. Could you stop at the station? I'll need a copy of your driver's license and fingerprints."

The chief stood up and walked him back to the Great Room. When he looked at his list for the next name, he noticed that Mark made eye contact with the bartender.

●●●

Meanwhile, C.J. was still talking to Joe Hardin, a nephew of Virginia's and son of her sister Carolina. Joe had had a few drinks and was very chatty. He could not stay on topic, so his answers were all over the place.

"Joe, how close were you to your Aunt Virginia?"

"Well, let me tell you C.G.," he slurred, "families are a funny thing. We are a family, but my mother and Virginia did not see eye to eye, so we rarely laid eyes on her ... ha, ha—get it? Anyway, we all live in the same town, so our paths did cross. My wife, Amelia, is a nurse at the hospital where Aunt Gin serves on the board. She saw her more than I did."

"Aunt Gin? Is that a family nickname?"

"Oh, did I say that? Well, you're going to find out sooner or later, Virginia liked her gin. The nickname wasn't used to her face."

C.J. looked up to see Ed already starting to interview two women. She needed to get this wrapped up. "So, Joe, what time did you get here?"

"We pulled up around half past three o'clock. Unloaded our suitcases. Seemed like someone should have been here to help with our luggage. In most places like this, a bellhop would meet the guests."

"Joe," C.J. interrupted, "did you see anyone?"

"Um, no. We went upstairs and found our room. Very nice, I must say. Have you ever been here? It's very tasteful..."

"Joe, did you and your wife stay in your room?"

"Well, Amelia did. I'm just not good with organization...

"Where did you go?"

"My drink is pretty low; can you wait until I get a refill?"

"Just answer the question, and we can talk again tomorrow."

Joe looked blank. C.J. repeated, "Where did you go?"

"Oh, I took the car over to the Lodge parking lot. I walked around the Lodge for a bit and came back around 4:45—in time for the Gather and Graze."

C.J. stood up, told Joe he could go, and went to see how the chief was doing. She jotted down in her notes that Joe had seemed pretty sincere about his arrival but couldn't account for the time between half past three and five o'clock.

7: IDENTICAL TWINS

C.J. found the chief with his hands full with two identical women, from the frosted tips of their brunette hair to their taupe velveteen pants suits, right down to their high-heeled open-toed shoes with cappuccino-lacquered toenails sticking out.

They were talking at the same time and each held her own bottle of Lambrusco. "Have a seat, ladies, and please let me have the spelling of your names," said Ed.

They spelled the same name twice, Elinore and Eleanor, and added that everyone called them Nora and Nelly.

Nelly and Nora might be talking at the same time, but they were talking about different things. "Look at this, Officer! See this corkscrew? It has red all over it and definitely could have cut Auntie's artery," Nelly said. She continued to swig the wine despite her notion that she had opened it with a corkscrew dipped in family blood.

Nora simultaneously was asking irrelevant questions. "Chiefy! Oh, Chiefy! Where's your favorite place to buy wine in this town? Give me that bottle, Nelly! Mine's empty."

"Go get your own bottle, you cow! That bartender over there can get you one. Why would I give you mine when I still have a full glass left in it—maybe."

Chief Ed and C.J. were swiveling back and forth at the bizarre conversation. The strangest thing about it was that Nelly and Nora could answer each other's statements before they were even finished uttering them. It was some weird version of identical twins reading each other's thoughts, and it was disconcertingly creepy.

Just as Ed was about to suggest that C.J. go with Nelly to the dining room, quicker than two cowboys drawing down in an old-time western, Nora shoved Nelly off balance. She hit the table hard enough to lose control of the wine that Nora was trying to get ahold of, dropping it on the hardwood floor and shattering it. More simultaneous name calling ensued as they assaulted one another with crustless cucumber sandwiches.

"Cow!"

"Slut!"

"Bitch!"

"Drunk!"

Ed shouted loud enough to catch the attention of the brawling sisters and said, "Our holding cell is small, but by God, you two can fit in it." He stuck his head out the door and told a patrolman to haul Nelly and Nora off to jail until they sobered up enough to be interviewed. "Charge both with assault for now. We can drop the charges if they come to their senses."

The twins left in the back of two squad cars, wearing matching handcuffs.

C.J. turned around in time to spot Mark having a conversation with the bartender and made a note of it.

•••

The Residenz just didn't look the same. Mary Ellen and Poppy were glad that Judy had left to take care of other business for now. Broken glass, spilled wine, and even an innocent platter of crustless cucumber sandwiches were everywhere. Clare stuck to her post in the kitchen. Poppy inspected the sandwiches, decided they wouldn't attract dogs, and started tossing them out. Mary Ellen caught this decision-making process out of the corner of her eye and said, "Good grief, Poppy. You're one short step away from dumpster diving."

Poppy said nothing since she still felt a little guilty about chasing a couple meatball subs that had fallen on hard times behind the local Subway. She caught two dogs with those subs, and they hadn't taken anything from the bottom line, she thought defensively.

But Mary Ellen and Poppy agreed on one thing when they had a chance to debrief. The entire rest of the family, both blood relatives and those by marriage, was completely unfazed by the twins' fight, the food on the floor, the wine all over, or even the sisters hauled off in handcuffs—and that, they concluded, wasn't normal. That wasn't even counting that one of their pack had been brutally murdered, and no one considered it as a random crime.

This was a very strange family. And they were all going to have a long night.

8: CLEANING UP

Clare, Mary Ellen, and Poppy started to clean up the mess. Clare asked, "Can one of you give me a ride home and a ride back up here in the morning?"

"I do have to get on those lost-dog cases—three dogs, missing from their homes. I'd like to get started first thing," answered Poppy.

"Can I help round up lost dogs for you, Poppy? You know I communicate well with dogs. It might help me not miss Cliff so much."

"Oh, Clare, this little town with its protective dog owners just doesn't have enough dogs for even me most weeks. I easily keep up with them by myself. I'm sorry. Those dogs are sort of my bread and butter. You might consider volunteering at the animal shelter instead."

"I'll think about it," Clare said. "But doing free work probably isn't a great option at the moment."

Mary Ellen had already left the kitchen. She had gone into the Great Room to pick up more dishes. As she walked by the staircase, she thought she might peek upstairs. The remaining family members were still finishing up drinks. As she reached the top of the stairs, she saw that one of the bedroom doors was open. The room was spacious, even including a king-sized bed. The bed had a cherry headboard, nightstands, and twin lamps. She walked in, and there was C.J.

C.J. looked at her quizzically. "May I help you?"

Mary Ellen decided to brave it out. "I was curious to see what the upstairs looked like." She knew C.J. was annoyed, but she didn't want to waste a chance to see the room that had been assigned to Virginia Stanley. The list on the table in the foyer had each family member's name and assigned room number. Mary Ellen knew her time was limited so she looked at as much of the room as she could. And sure enough, C.J. told her to leave as this was an active murder investigation.

Mary Ellen hurried downstairs and went back into the kitchen. Poppy said, "Where were you? Can you pick up Clare tomorrow and bring her up here in the morning?"

"Sure. But listen. I just went upstairs. C.J. was in Virginia's bedroom, and I only had a second, but it appears there is a file folder on the dresser. It's labeled 'Important Papers.' I didn't get to see what was in it, but I bet Ed and C.J. will have a better handle on the family."

Since Clare was still hiding in the kitchen, Poppy made one last trip to the dining room, where Ed was talking to Ned, the other nephew. Ned was taller than his cousin, nice looking, well dressed, but had a decidedly whiny voice. He was explaining that his mother was Virginia Stanley's other sister, Dakota. He laughed and said, "They were known as the States of Stanley, as they all had state names."

Ed asked, "What time did you get to the Residenz?"

Ned thought for a moment. "Not exactly sure, but in time to walk Aunt Virginia out to the carriage. I was telling her how grateful we were to be invited and how much we were looking forward to a nice time. Then I told the carriage driver to have her back at five o'clock sharp. He's a suspicious character, I must say. I hope you're keeping an eye on him. Just seems shady," Ned sniffed.

Ed looked up to see Poppy stacking dishes and platters very slowly. He cleared his throat. "Hope you got all that, Poppy. But I do need you to go back to the kitchen. These are not public interviews."

Poppy tried unsuccessfully to look embarrassed, picked up the dishes, and pushed open the kitchen door. Meanwhile, Mary Ellen was trying to clean up the Great Room as best she could. The room was a mess, and no one seemed to care. Glasses sat on tables with no coasters, food scraps dotted the coffee table, and crumbs were all over the floor. The professional cleaners would have to finish the job tomorrow.

•••

Ed sat down with Joe's wife, Amelia, and asked, "What is your job?"

"I'm a nurse at the hospital, specializing in pain management," she said.

Ed continued, "After you arrived this afternoon, what did you do?"

"Well, we went to our room, and I unpacked. I came down around 4:45? I was on the veranda when the carriage pulled up," she shuddered.

"OK," said Ed. "Send Arrabella to see me, please."

Amelia came back shortly and said, "Chief, Arrabella went to bed."

Mary Ellen bustled back through to the kitchen. Poppy and Clare were ready to leave, so they closed the door behind them and headed home.

9: ROSCŒ, CHUCKIE, AND MUNCHIE

Poppy woke up early the next day and had no intention of using any of the time to help out in the kitchen over at the Residenz. Clare ought to be able to handle herself if Mary Ellen gave her a ride, plus Clare needed to figure out how to get around town without them. Poppy was focused on dog chasing.

First things first, though—she really needed some coffee, and knew that Sharon B., and the other Sharon B., and possibly the third Sharon B. in town might also be having a cup. She could use the caffeine and the conversation.

She walked into the Harvest and sure enough there were the Sharons, all three of them. They made room right away, figuring Poppy might know something about an actual murder in town—something that struck everyone as almost impossible. Poppy confirmed it though. "I wish I could say it was just another tourist with a heart attack, but the inside of that buggy had blood everywhere where a major artery pulsed out. Mary Ellen and I'll get together again and see what we can figure out around noon. Meantime, has anyone seen Roscoe, Chuckie, or Munchie?"

"Good grief," Sharon said. "Why are all the dogs running around loose? I did think I might have seen Munchie heading down through the park toward the river, though."

"Really?" Poppy seemed hopeful by the lead. "I'm guessing I can find Chuckie hanging around the school, but I don't have a clue about the other two."

"Who is Munchie? Is that a Jenniches dog?" asked another Sharon.

Poppy explained, "No Jenniches dog leaves home. Best trained dogs in town."

"Better than Babycakes?" quipped the third Sharon, and the whole place laughed.

"Don't forget to check with the police. You know how good they are about hanging onto someone's dog for a while to give them time to come fetch them," said Sharon.

"True. And I'll find out. Sadly, though, if the police have found the dog, there goes my finder's fee."

"Why wouldn't the dogs just go home? Don't they want breakfast or something?" asked another Sharon B., one who wasn't into family dogs.

"Wouldn't you think? But every dog is always looking out for his worst interest," said Poppy. "T.S. Eliot had it backwards. A dog is not a cat. I better get going."

"Wait," said Sharon. "You haven't mentioned how things are going with you and Jack."

"Oh, there's nothing to tell." Poppy waved her off.

"Already?" all three Sharons said at once.

"He eats sunflower seeds like a gerbil. They are everywhere. It was a bad idea to think anything could come of that. But! That's in the past now."

They marveled at how quickly Poppy's latest interest always slid into the past tense. And they also marveled at the whole sunflower seeds thing since Poppy herself wasn't all that dedicated to perfection, as her car famously attested. Too many dogs, too little time for cleaning it out when you were going to dump another stray in quickly. Poppy, herself aware of the inconsistency but not caring, grabbed her key fob off the table and headed out.

•••

Just as she was reversing out of the parking spot, she slammed on her brakes. Who did she see in the backup camera? It was Roscoe—none other than. She threw her van in park, grabbed a leash and the bag of deli food she had "cleaned up" last night, and jumped out of the car.

"Roscoe! Hey, Roscoe! Here, boy! Look what I have here—I have roast beef!"

Roscoe stopped short. He looked at Poppy with his big Rottweiler eyes but didn't move toward her. Poppy knew he had to puzzle this out himself. Even the best-kept dog didn't get a choice on where to live and had a curiosity that made "freedom" attractive.

But he smelled food, and he was a dog inclined to make friends, so her talking softly to him was an attraction, too.

"Come on over here, Roscoe," Poppy cooed softly. "You know freedom's just another word for nothing left to lose. Janis was right. And here's something you want. Roast beef," she continued, knowing he had been out all night. Freedom vs. breakfast. Poppy had to rely on enticing dogs to give up rare moments of freedom in exchange for other attractions.

She knew better than to reach for him, so she held out some roast beef instead. The indecision drained from his face, and he closed the last six feet between them without hesitation.

Poppy gave him the big chunk of roast beef sandwich, checking to make sure it wasn't loaded with horseradish. As he took it out of her left hand, she slipped the leash onto his collar with her right and opened the van door for him, tossing in a second piece of roast beef. Roscoe hopped in the car like Keith Richards catching an Uber back to his hotel.

She drove him home and, bam! One dog who was lost was found. The whole process, positive for Roscoe, would make it that much easier to get him in her car next time. Next time was almost guaranteed.

●●●

Poppy had a feeling about and a lot of experience with Chuckie; she headed over to the elementary school. Chuckie was a toy poodle with a bad attitude who would bite anyone. He was well known and anyone thinking of greeting Chuckie hesitated, wondering if this was one of his biting days.

Not for the first time, Poppy wondered what a little stability might do for Chuckie. Toy poodles, while perhaps not the world's friendliest dogs, weren't on the run very much either. And they bonded tightly with their person. So, what was going on with Chuckie? Apparently, when his kid, Marcia, headed off to school, Chuckie went into high-anxiety mode.

To the uninitiated, he might look innocent and, while he might bite, he was no killer. But there weren't that many uninitiated left in town when it came to Chuckie. People took the long way around him when he was off on an "adventure."

Poppy found him exactly where she expected to—in front of the elementary school where Marcia was in third grade. Look at that dog bouncing around outside the door, thought Poppy. He's looking to slip in if anyone opens it. Unlike Roscoe, Chuckie was on a very specific mission and wouldn't be easily dissuaded by a piece of roast beef. Poppy put on heavy-duty gloves for the occasion—they were pretty much her Chuckie Gloves. She thought that might be a great brand name for dog-catching gloves.

Just as Chuckie was making his way toward the door in earnest because he spotted someone who might be leaving, Poppy reached down and swooped him up in her gloved hands.

This happened at the same time a student teacher opened the door for an outside break. He spotted Poppy and Chuckie. "Whoa! Do you need some help there?" he asked Poppy. "Is that a poodle or a Tasmanian devil?"

"This—this guy right here," Poppy started to respond, having to raise her voice to be heard over Chuckie's snarling, growling, and snapping, "is just Chuckie." She laughed. "And he wants to find Marcia."

Chuckie was showing signs of fatigue. He'd been out for ages, hadn't had breakfast, and hadn't found Marcia—and now he was being handled by Poppy.

Poppy tossed Chuckie into the back seat, where a chunk of roast beef sandwich awaited him. He sat next to the sandwich, ignoring it. "Don't worry, Chuck," Poppy said. "No one will think less of you for eating that sandwich." He took a sniff and a lick and finally started chewing, punctuated by an occasional growl at Poppy. This is a dog, thought Poppy, who doesn't trust anyone.

When Poppy dropped him off, she did notice he got a lackluster greeting from his owner, who said, "Uh, thanks for finding him again."

"He's in the same spot every time," said Poppy. "The school. You could just run over and save yourself my fee."

"He might bite me," she said.

"Make up reasons to tell him what a good dog he is," began Poppy, thinking she might also run away from this house. "Dogs respond quickly to praise and ..." But the door slammed in her face. At least Chuckie wouldn't get run over by a school-bus driver who couldn't even see him. Time to go find the much more elusive Munchie.

•••

Two out of three. Poppy was closing in on a trifecta, with one dog to go. Roscoe and Chuckie took a total of fifteen minutes to return home.

So, Sharon (or was it Sharon?) had recalled seeing Munchie head over toward the river behind the Lodge and not far at all from the Residenz, where no doubt investigations were continuing.

Munchie was easy. A big, mixed-breed galoot with long black-and-white hair, he would run and greet anyone who knew his name, or really, anyone. If you could find him, you could catch him, in Poppy's experience. He might very well knock you over as he misjudged the distance in a final leap to greet you, but at least you didn't have to chase him.

Munchie heard Poppy before he saw her. He swiveled his big, square head and floppy ears nearly 180 degrees to eyeball Poppy.

He had been gone overnight, and he smelled food coming from Poppy's direction. He picked up the prize he had been carrying back from the river and made toward Poppy with his find, on a dead run. At the last second, she tried to swerve but it was impossible to out-time Munchie.

She went down hard, flat on her back, an easy maneuver for Munchie, but Poppy had the element of surprise when she reached up and got the leash on him. "Gotcha, Munchie. Your people are looking for you."

Munchie let go of his prize, and the human hand, severed just above the wrist, dropped down practically on Poppy's chin. She picked up her phone and called 911.

10: THE FAMILY ALBUM

Mary Ellen got up early and wandered into her kitchen. Her husband, Todd, was filling up the Keurig for their morning coffee.

"Don't worry about me," Mary Ellen said. "I have to go back to the Residenz with Clare this morning, then drop her off to pick up her van."

"We aren't Uber drivers, are we?" asked Todd kiddingly.

Mary Ellen gave him a quick kiss and hurried out the door. The weather had turned beautiful and even though it was late fall, it made her happy to put the top down on the convertible.

She picked up Clare about five minutes later. Clare looked surprised that the top was down, but she was grateful for the ride. Mary Ellen had turned up the heat, so it wasn't terribly uncomfortable. As they drove toward town, Mary Ellen suggested they stop and grab a takeout coffee at the Harvest. She needed her coffee fix.

They pulled into the Residenz parking lot, ready to work and hopefully learn something. The catering cleanup was just beginning. Clare had brought along towels to wrap her dishes in so they wouldn't get chipped or broken in transit.

"Looks like everything is well organized. I'm going to wrap these dishes myself, if you don't mind. I'm used to doing it, and I have a method," said Clare.

Mary Ellen peeked into the dining room. "Looks like the whole family has assembled," she said, "including the twins."

Clare finished wrapping her platters and looked ready to load them in the car. Mary Ellen walked over to open the door when Clare stopped. "Darn, I have to go upstairs."

Mary Ellen looked surprised. "Upstairs?"

"Some of my little dessert plates are in the bedrooms. I brought them up early yesterday filled with sweet treats. It'll just take a second. I have a master key."

Clare started out the door and realized the whole family was gathered at the table and likely to see her. She backed into the kitchen. Mary Ellen realized the problem immediately.

"I'll go out and distract them while you hustle by."

With that said, Mary Ellen pushed open the door and greeted everyone with a cheery, "Good morning."

Everyone looked a bit startled.

"I'm Mary Ellen. I was here last night helping the caterer. I'm just back to pick up some dishes. Are those family albums you have? How interesting."

Nora and Nelly, who were each holding an album, said in unison, "Family albums for a family reunion." While still identically dressed, they looked quite put together and didn't seem at all embarrassed that this stranger probably saw their terrible behavior the night before.

Nora, or maybe Nelly, said, "Our mother and Joe's mother had all the family photos. They had arranged them by dates and family groupings. After the sisters fell out, we didn't have many pictures of Aunt Gin. Really just newspaper articles."

Ned pointed at one of the pictures. "There's Joe opening his Radio Shack store and another of Joe opening his Blockbuster store. No wonder Gin didn't want to fund another business opportunity for you."

Joe turned red and retorted, "Just like there was going to be no funding for a play starring Arrabella."

Mary Ellen wanted to leave before things got ugly even though it seemed as if this exchange was not new business. Fortunately, she glanced up the stairs to see Clare walking down with her little plates.

Suddenly, Nelly or Nora jumped up and exclaimed, "Maris, is that you? Oh, my goodness. We wondered where you had gone."

Clare/Maris said, "Actually I'm Clare's Catering now. I've been trying to get my business off the ground here in Frankenmuth." Her voice, despite her best efforts, quavered.

The family all looked around the table and a twin said, "Guys, we owe her. Aunt Gin ruined her business. We all agreed to stay as the trip was prepaid. We need to have her do another meal for us." They looked at Clare/Maris. "Could you do dinner for us? Something simple? Maybe a cookout-type thing, casual? There's a firepit outside." Everyone was nodding and smiling.

"Would tonight work?" Clare asked. "It's a decent day and outside would be pleasant. I'll get the Lodge to send over some heat lamps and tables. Fingers crossed Judy will okay this."

Ned said, "She has been remarkably generous to us. I'm sure there will be no problem."

Mary Ellen asked, "Just curious, how did you recognize Clare? She only catered for your aunt once and that didn't end well."

Ned smiled. "Nelly and Nora have this facial recognition thing. If they see you once, they will recall who you are and where they know you from. They are extremely bright, despite what you may think. They own a wildly successful financial planning firm."

The twins smiled and said together, "We work hard and play harder."

Clare and Mary Ellen said their goodbyes. Clare needed to get her menu together and Mary Ellen was hoping her favorite mah-jongg group was at the coffee house, ready to break walls. Clare managed to get Mary Ellen to commit that she and Poppy would help with the barbecue before she took off.

11: THE SCOOP FROM LIBERTY

C.J. was sitting in the break room with a steaming cup of coffee when Ed walked into the police station.

"Good morning," she said. "I just took the twins back up to the Residenz. This morning the girls woke up and apologized for their behavior. Evidently, they work hard and play harder. I told them we'd be up there later to continue their interview. Just emailed the police chief in Liberty, Ohio, for some background on the Stanley family."

"Thanks, C.J. Buddy and Tom should be here momentarily. Let's meet in the conference room."

The email from the Liberty police department was already in Ed's inbox. He called Judy at the Lodge and arranged to send an officer to talk to each Residenz staff member who had been working the day before.

By the time he walked into the conference room, C.J., Buddy, and Tom were seated with notebooks and coffee. Ed pulled up a chair.

"Yesterday, Virginia Stanley left the Residenz in a Heritage carriage driven by Mark Thomas of Birch Run," he said. "He has worked for Heritage for ten years. At this point we have found no connection between Mark and the victim. However, she died in his carriage during the ride. He'll stop by today for fingerprints. If I'm not here, have him run through his story again. We'll check it against what he told me last night.

"We need to nail down where they were between four o'clock and five o'clock yesterday. C.J. and I will handle that. Buddy and Tom, how did you make out?"

"We drove the usual carriage route, knocked on some doors, and asked some locals what they saw. Everyone sees the carriages, but nobody really sees them, you know what I mean? It was rainy, so there weren't many locals out walking, and not many people sitting outside."

"Okay, so today, go to Heritage Carriage and talk to some of the other drivers. Then next, go to the Lodge. Judy will have a list of employees for you to speak with. Questions?"

Both officers shook their heads and stood up, ready to get started.

"Wait, before you go, let me share this email from the chief down in Liberty. He said the Stanley family is prominent in town. They made their money in stainless steel. The patriarch started the company in the 1920s. They expanded as the years went by, eventually specializing in medical instruments. Virginia's father sold the business, making the family quite wealthy. Virginia was a philanthropist and gave generously to causes she approved of. Joe and Amelia live in town. He has owned several businesses, and she is a nurse. The twins, Elinore and Eleanor," he looked up, "same name, different spelling, are financial planners, also in Liberty. Ned has recently moved back to town. Before he moved, he was a jack of all trades. Chief said to call him if we need any more information."

He looked over at C.J. "Anything else to add?"

"Yes. Last night, I went upstairs to look in Virginia's room. There was a folder on the dresser labeled 'Important Papers.' Several of the papers came from a private investigator who had researched the nieces and nephews. Pretty interesting stuff. Joe and Amelia are in financial crisis and about to lose their house. Joe has started to look into acquiring a Skyline Chili franchise. The twins do have a financial planning business that is quite successful, but they have had a filing against them from the SEC. This has not been made public. Ned has just moved back to town with hopes of raising money to fund a play he wrote that will feature his fiancé. The PI hadn't checked her out yet. Virginia's will was also in the folder. I think that should probably be looked at by an attorney."

"Very interesting. Guys, you get started. C.J. and I will be at the Residenz."

Just then, the front desk officer knocked and stuck his head in the door. "Chief, Poppy just called in. She needs a hand over on the riverbank; actually she said she had a hand, but that seems pretty unlikely."

"Thanks. C.J., change of plans. Let's go see what Poppy needs."

12: MUNCHIE DROPS A CLUE

Ed and C.J. drove close to the river, where they saw Poppy standing outside her car and Munchie on a leash. Nothing looked out of control, and they were having a hard time imagining what sort of help she needed.

Poppy said, "Do you have evidence bags? I told whoever answered the phone that you should bring some."

Ed responded that there were always bags in the vehicle, and asked, "For what, Poppy? What did you find?"

Poppy gave credit where it was due and told him Munchie had a prize, pointing a few feet in front of her.

"Whoa," C.J. said. "We were told you needed a hand, not that you had an extra one."

Poppy described her encounter with Munchie and his giving her a hand—smack on her chin. "Talk about disgusting," Poppy continued. "I called and stood guard here—although I'll need to get Munchie home soon, but I didn't want other critters or weirdos making off with this hand. Do you think it has anything to do with yesterday's murder of Virginia?"

"We've got no idea yet, Poppy. We'll see what we find.

Thank you for calling and staying with the … the hand here."
Ed frowned. "This is the first significant body part ever found
lying around a city park—not counting a tooth, for example,
or the rare fingertip from an old woodcarver."

Meantime, C.J. had called for a cadaver dog, and here
he and his handler were now. Munchie howled a friendly
greeting to Teddy, who seemed not to hear him. Poppy put
Munchie in her car and took off toward the List house.

Usually, Teddy's handler only had chances to show up in
schools and have Teddy demonstrate how he could quickly
find a stash of pot. He gave the hand a sniff and took off
straight away toward the riverbank. He headed east about a
quarter of a mile and signaled a find. The three police officers
were right behind him and saw the body partly submerged
in the shallows. Both arms were floating toward the surface
with the right one looking, well, short.

Everyone knew the drill now. The forensic team showed
up and did its thing.

Both Ed and C.J. were pretty positive, even face down,
who this was. C.J. looked at Ed and said, "Mark." Ed nodded.
Indeed, it was the body of the carriage driver, oddly missing
the one hand.

Back at the police station, it was all hands—so to speak—
on deck with C.J. at the whiteboard. "What have we got, and
what does it mean?" C.J. asked. Everyone brainstormed:

VIRGINIA (DEAD) FOUND IN
MARK'S CARRIAGE

MARK—ONLY PERSON ON
SCENE—PRIME SUSPECT

NIECES AND NEPHEWS—SECONDARY
SUSPECTS: GRUDGES? MONEY?

QUESTION: WHY KILL MARK?

QUESTION: WAS MARK'S MURDER
UNRELATED TO VIRGINIA'S?

QUESTION: WHY CUT OFF MARK'S HAND?

QUESTION: WASN'T IT STILL POSSIBLE
MARK KILLED VIRGINIA?

QUESTION: HOW MANY KILLERS DO WE
HAVE ROAMING FRANKENMUTH?

C.J. summarized. "Our prime suspect is now dead. But does that mean he had nothing to do with Virginia's death, or does it seem even more likely that he had some role in her death? Clare, as far as we know, is still unaware that we know she had a motive. With the entire clan having talked to Clare now, several of them have tipped us off about the grudge—a chance to point the finger outside the family circle."

Ed took over. "We don't have a lot of people we can assign to this case since the normal Frankenmuth policing still needs to continue, more than ever. So, C.J. will coordinate assignments.

"But we aren't going to ignore other resources we have available. We're going to ask Mary Ellen and Poppy—no groaning now!—they are usually anxious to help, even though nothing this serious has happened before—to work the streets, so to speak, for what they can learn from their remarkably complex grapevine. Did someone snort? Now, no snorting. Let's face it, they have more time than the rest of us to just hang out and compare information with lots of people in town. So that's it. Everyone be good to Mary Ellen and Poppy. Yes, even me. I heard that back there."

"Everyone be back in this room, please, in twenty-four hours to see if we've got any answers to those questions," said C.J.

"Hey! I heard that," said Ed in the general direction of someone muttering that the place was going to the dogs. "It was one of Poppy's lost dogs, Munchie—you guys all know Munchie—who literally spit out Mark's hand, a freaking body part, right on Poppy. I call that delivering the goods. See what you can find out."

"Dismissed!" Ed picked up a bottle of Tums and tossed back a handful. Maybe bodies really were going to start falling all over Frankenmuth.

13: MAHJ MAVEN

Mary Ellen dropped Clare off and headed home to check in with Todd before she went downtown to play mah-jongg. Todd was standing in the kitchen, making himself a sandwich.

"Welcome home," said Todd. "Want half?" he offered, holding out a bologna and cheese. Mary Ellen gratefully took the sandwich and then told Todd all about the bizarre Stanley family and the dead matriarch.

Todd frowned, "Are you and Poppy in over your heads? This may get dangerous. I really don't like it, M.E."

"Actually, we're fine. Ed is on the case and it's just a family picnic." But inside, she wasn't really sure that she shouldn't be a little worried. Well, she and Poppy would have to keep their wits about them. With a jaunty wave, she walked to the door. Over her shoulder, she reminded Todd it was mah-jongg day.

Todd waved back and said, "Every day is a mah-jongg day in M.E.'s world."

As Mary Ellen got into her car, she remembered she hadn't told Todd she would be helping Clare again that evening. She turned to go back inside but decided in light of Todd's admonition, a text later in the day might be the best solution.

As she pulled into the coffee house parking lot, she noticed several cars she recognized as belonging to her mah-jongg friends. This was a great group of like-minded aficionados of the game. There were no cliques, just a mission to have fun … and sometimes win a few quarters.

Several years ago, a neighbor, Pat M., had told Mary Ellen about a game they played in Florida where she wintered. Mah-jongg, a game invented in China and adapted to an American form, was played with tiles and a yearly card that had the hands needed to win a game. Mary Ellen fell in love immediately and studied cards, websites, blogs, and played online. As a result, she became the Maven of the Muth and taught other people how to play. As the ex-librarian at the Wickson Library, she wanted to play there. The current librarian, Pam W., was delighted to have an adult activity in the upstairs space and even bought a set of tiles that could be checked out.

•••

Today, they were at the coffee shop. It was always nice to have a cappuccino to enjoy as the tiles went up on the rack. As she walked in and looked up, she could see two tables, one of four and one of three. Perfect, a spot with her name on it.

The group greeted her enthusiastically, changing quickly from a game of three to four. It was an easy change. Walls were broken and tiles claimed. Mary Ellen quickly put her tiles on her rack and organized them by suit. She inwardly groaned. No jokers or obvious trends. It was not going to be easy to find a winning hand.

As everyone got organized and looked up from their racks, Sue P. casually asked, "Does anyone know anything about a murder at the Residenz? I heard someone in town mention it, but I couldn't quite wrap my head around a murder in Frankenmuth."

Mary Ellen looked up. She was tempted to share what she knew, but thought maybe this news would be better told when there was more solid information. She realized she hadn't heard from Poppy all day.

Mary C. cleared her throat and looked at Mary Ellen. Evidently, they had all been waiting on her to play. With this hand, her path forward needed her full attention. It didn't take Mary C. long to declare "mah-jongg." Quarters were handed down the table. Mary C. was a gracious winner. She should be—she had plenty of practice.

The coffee house was a busy place. Mary Ellen couldn't help but notice when one of the regulars walked in and loudly placed her order. Maisie had a successful cleaning business. When she cleaned your house, it sparkled. She also had one of those voices that carried, so everyone could hear what she had to say. Today was no different.

"Did you hear about the murder in the pony carriage? Some old tourist lady was found murdered. Chief Ed and his people had better catch that murderer. Are we safe in our own beds?"

They all made eye contact. Sometimes Maisie had incorrect information, but because Sue P. had already heard this, the group looked interested and a little alarmed. Mary Ellen decided sharing at this point would not be useful.

"And I saw a carriage stopping up near Frankenmuth Florist," Maisie continued. "Didn't know carriages ran errands. That business better tighten their routes if they don't want to lose trade. You know how word gets around."

Everyone in the place knew how it got around—mostly Maisie spread it. As much as she wanted to play more mahjongg, Mary Ellen decided it was time to text Poppy. Just as she picked up her phone, Poppy texted her.

"Coming to the Harvest—don't move!"

Mary Ellen excused herself from her friends and went down the stairs. "Good luck, and remember—you can never use a joker with a pair."

She heard Kathy T. groan, "Why, why, why?"

14: CHEESE MAN

Poppy enjoyed playing mah-jongg when she could, but didn't have Mary Ellen's passion/obsession with the game, although she loved the social aspect. But this morning, rounding up dogs took up her time. When she finally arrived at the Harvest, the Sharons and everyone else but Mary Ellen had gone on to other things.

Mary Ellen, though, had claimed one of two tiny outdoor tables by the sidewalk right across Main Street from the enormous and relatively new Cheese Haus. She had Poppy's favorite drink waiting. Poppy quickly caught her up on Munchie's find, including the fact that there was a second body down by the river, separated from its hand. "And we know that guy. It's Mark, the buggy driver."

"Holy crap!"

Right about this time, an older man of indeterminate age was strolling down the street toward the coffee house. He looked like a stepped-down generation from Col. Sanders of chicken fame, kind of ironic since far better chicken was the main dish that made Frankenmuth famous. You didn't leave town to get chicken in Frankenmuth.

•••

The strolling man was a visitor, Adam Brown, who hailed from Ohio, home of a large tourist pool for the town. Adam looked preoccupied today. For one thing, he was in town to conduct business with management at the Cheese Haus, to get a few brands and types of cheese he represented from northern Ohio into the lineup of hundreds of cheeses they sold. He hoped the Cheese Haus was expansive enough to be open to the choices he offered.

And what Adam offered would be more along the line of a variety of flavored Cheese Whizzes, if one could picture it. Whipped bland cheese with horseradish, whipped bland cheese with jalapeños, and whipped bland cheese with cinnamon, because there was a whipped bland cheese in Adam's sample case for every taste. Frankenmuth was not a snooty town either—if people wanted whipped bland cheese with cinnamon, if Adam could show there was a market, then whipped bland cheese with cinnamon would find a home there.

Adam looked at his watch and entered the Cheese Haus to meet with the cheese buyer. He allowed thirty minutes for it until his next appointment. But Adam found himself back on the street in ten. The confident buyer in the trademark dirndl dress had ended the conversation by calmly saying, "I'm sorry, Mr. Brown. Your products simply aren't a good match for our inventory."

He leaned against the giant mouse outside the Haus with his briefcase full of Cheese Whiz samples and calmed down. "Women," he muttered, "don't know a good business proposition!"

•••

Something about the stranger caused Poppy and Mary Ellen to interrupt their train of thought. Was it the uncanny resemblance to Col. Sanders? Mary Ellen said, "Who's that guy? Do we know him, or is he just another tourist who's enjoyed the sample cheese?"

Poppy said, "Oh, he's obviously a tourist making the rounds. Should we go offer to take his picture with the mouse? You know how everyone loves to have their photo with Klaus—it's almost like he's Mickey."

"Sure," said Mary Ellen. Just as they were getting up from their chairs to be good representatives of their town, a 1999 Diamond Edition Lincoln Continental pulled into the Harvest parking lot, with Betty Wray steering the ship. Betty Wray was a former fashion model and still beautiful at ninety-two. They waved and when they looked back across the street, they noticed one of the twins—nieces of Virginia's—making a beeline for Adam. They embraced, too long to be just friends, causing Mary Ellen and Poppy to ease themselves back into their chairs.

"That guy wasn't at the Residenz, was he?" asked Poppy.

"Nope. I would have remembered him."

Poppy took out her cellphone and surreptitiously took a photo of the couple, who then headed to the parking lot by the river in back of the Cheese Haus. "It's not every day you get a picture of Col. Sanders." They laughed.

"We need to see if we can figure out what exactly happened to Mark. Let's just file this observation under something odd and follow up later," said Mary Ellen.

Poppy agreed. "Mark's been around this town for a long time. Let's see what our sources know about him that could help the police."

And off they went.

15: THE MAYOR CONFERS WITH THE CHIEF

"I've got urgent news for you, M.A.A. Please give me a ring ASAP." Ed hung up and turned to the mess of papers on his desk. Mary Anne Ackerman, mayor of Frankenmuth (M.A.A. to her long-time acquaintances), always worked to get out ahead of the news. This was the biggest deal in Frankenmuth since the flood of 1986.

Ed had used the word "urgent," hoping to set the tone of the call. He started to move the papers on his desk. His office door opened, and Buddy and Tom walked in.

"Chief, we're back from the Lodge."

Ed interrupted, "Wait a minute. This desk is a disaster; this leads to sloppy police work. We have a system here. All reports should be in a labeled folder and placed in the inbox."

Tom had sidled over to the desk to scoop up some of the offending papers. He looked around the office until Ed offered him a folder and a label.

"Sorry, Chief."

Buddy cleared his throat.

"Judy had the staff's employment papers ready for us when we got there. Several maids had been sent up to the Residenz in the morning. Nothing jumped out about them and they were gone by noon, so we didn't interview them."

Tom added, "The bartender is low priority because there appears to be no connection other than his work."

"Did you talk to him?"

Both officers shook their heads. Buddy said, "He's working later today if we need to interview him."

"I'll call Judy and see where he's working tonight," said Ed. "Thanks, guys. Now, could you do a deep dive on Mark Thomas? We need to know why he was killed."

Both officers looked puzzled. "Oh, right," said Ed. "You missed the latest update. Mark Thomas, our carriage driver, was found dead this morning. Poppy and one of her errant dogs found him, or rather found his hand, which led to the discovery of his body in the river. Now, this is police business, so get all the information you can without divulging why you need it, understand? We need to delay the headline on MLive until we get a better handle on this."

As the young men turned to leave, M.A.A. showed up at the door in one of her dirndls that she wore for official business. On the mayor, a dirndl looked culturally appropriate, not like a costume. Ed shut the door behind them. "Well?" M.A.A. asked. "Urgent? News?"

"Actually, yes. We've had two murders in Frankenmuth in the past two days. The first, an older lady, Virginia Stanley, who took a carriage ride and on the return to the Residenz was discovered to be dead. I assume Judy has already told you about that."

M.A.A. nodded.

Ed continued, "This morning, Poppy found a hand while chasing Munchie." There was no need to identify either Poppy or Munchie to M.A.A., as they were all neighbors.

"What!" exclaimed M.A.A.

Ed continued, "The hand belonged to Mark Thomas, a local carriage driver, and the carriage driver of Virginia Stanley, the other dead body. The rest of Mark was found in the river. Bridgeport is working on time and method of death. We are working under the assumption that both murders are connected.

"At some point, the press will have to be advised. It might be good if we do a joint news release. Hopefully, we can stall a news conference until we have more information."

"First, Ed, is there any chance that the community is in danger? If there is the slightest chance that anyone living in Frankenmuth or visiting should feel afraid, that is unacceptable."

"M.A.A., I feel strongly that these cases are related, and the general public is not in harm's way."

M.A.A. shook her head. "Hope this doesn't come back to haunt us."

16: NEWS AT 6:00

Poppy and Babycakes were glued to the TV at the same time. Well, Poppy was glued to the TV, and Babycakes was glued to Poppy.

Babycakes was adopted through Midwest Boston Terrier Rescue and like many rescue dogs, went through an array of difficulties before her soft landing. Poppy always marveled when holding her at how well-nourished she looked—having doubled her emaciated adoption weight—at what a gorgeous, healthy coat thick enough to shed all over she had, and at how Babycakes had developed that sense of ownership of her space. The two of them were a small pack, but a pack nonetheless.

Independently, Poppy, and not so much Babycakes, was struck by the number of out-of-county press that showed up from Detroit. Mayor M.A.A. stepped smoothly in front of the microphones. She was in her comfort zone talking to the press, but missing her trademark smile under the circumstances. Chief Ed and C.J. stood back from the microphones.

The mayor kept her part short. "Good evening. I'm Mayor Mary Anne Ackerman. We have, as you've heard, had a very unusual situation in Frankenmuth with two murders in two days. We do not believe that the general public is in danger in town, and, between our police and the Michigan State police, everything possible is being done to bring about an arrest in these cases. Now I'm going to turn this press conference over to Chief Ed Swartz, who can fill you in on where we are and what's being done, and take a few questions."

The chief stepped forward and kept details to a minimum. He did not mention the disembodied hand, hoping that not many people knew about that yet. He did explain that Virginia was murdered while in a tourist carriage and that the driver was murdered the next day and found in the river. They had a "number of leads" but he encouraged the public to come forward to the police with anything at all they might believe to be relevant. He finished with, "I'll take a couple questions."

The Detroit Free Press reporter pole-vaulted her question first, like the pro she was. "What makes you think the general public isn't in danger? Do you think you have one murderer, two, or more roaming among the tourists undiscovered?"

The chief responded, "We aren't in a position to comment on those points now, other than to say we think it is more likely one killer with specific motives, and we will let you know more as soon as we can." The Free Press wasn't happy with that. Ed was fully aware that the reporter didn't feel this was responsive, and Ed himself wanted off this stage as soon as possible. But he figured now that he had addressed the big-time press, the worst was over.

But Ed figured wrong.

Of absolute necessity, Ed gave the nod to the local newspaper, a weekly that had a crime beat as part of its normal reporting. That consisted almost entirely of drunk drivers causing accidents, old people accidentally driving through the doors of Rite-Aid, and some shoplifting apprehensions. On a bad week, there might be some gnome vandalism by the local youths. Ed was convinced he would get a softball question and be off the stage in another thirty seconds.

But the paper's crime beat reporter chirped up with, "Can you confirm that the body of the carriage driver was mutilated, and have you determined whether a local dog named Munchie removed the hand from the body himself? And how would this possibly be connected to the first murder that seems nothing like this one? Or do you also have a killer dog on the loose in addition to at least one murderer?"

The chief had a long moment of disbelief combined with irritation, and finally said the safest thing he could think of. "I cannot comment on any of that. We haven't gotten a full forensics analysis back yet. Thanks for your time, everyone." And with that, he was off the stage.

Mayor Ackerman was waiting for him. "We need a higher police presence, using every marked vehicle in town, to make the tourists feel safer."

"Will see what I can do, M.A.A.," Ed said.

Meanwhile, the camera closed in on the WNEM local reporter, who said, "Well! You heard it here. An escalation in technique? Or a killing by a local pet who had escaped from home? One killer human on the first murder, and one mad dog for the second one? Or is Munchie the Dog merely a coincidence? And why is that dog named Munchie anyway? The chief neither admitted nor denied how many killers there are in this town, whether human or canine."

"Thank you, Sally," said the in-studio anchor. He smiled at the camera and said, "Time for our local forecast! We have a little weather ahead—specifics after this break."

Babycakes had reacted both times Munchie's name was spoken by turning her ears toward the TV. Otherwise, she didn't look impressed.

But Poppy was thunderstruck that the local reporter had spilled all the secrets that the police had hoped to hold back for a while. And she was a little concerned for Munchie's safety. One could walk away from this press conference thinking that at least two killers were loose in the city, as well as one possible mad dog. This wasn't good.

●●●

Judy watched from her executive office at the Lodge, working long hours as always, and worried that this could put a dent in the chicken-dinner count. They needed to catch someone quickly and put an end to this speculation. She also wondered if their own town reporter might have been a little over-the-top aggressive.

The Detroit reporter thought she had a great story that would be of considerable interest, and she picked up the phone to make reservations for the next few days at the Lodge.

Clare had a sense of dread, wondering if the Stanleys would disrupt her life yet again, just as she was establishing herself there.

The Cheese Man and a twin watched together from bed and reached for some Cheese Whiz and crackers, jalapeño flavored.

Ed said, "Crap."

And one of the mah-jongg players, Karen, turned to her husband, Rick, and said, "Have you seen Munchie?"

Rick responded, "I thought he was with you in the kitchen."

Munchie for his part had had a long day, was glad to be home for once, and was sound asleep in Karen and Rick's bed, having no idea he was a dog of interest.

17: THE FAMILY BARBECUE

While Todd cleaned up the dishes from dinner, Mary Ellen went to change into warmer clothes. She was just about ready to leave when he said, "So, did you forget to tell me about the dismembered body?"

Usually, Todd and Mary Ellen ate at seven o'clock and watched Jeopardy. Mary Ellen was especially fond of the Final Jeopardy part each night, always yelling woohoo! when she was correct. Tonight, they had eaten at five o'clock because of the barbecue. Mary Ellen had then turned on the TV, having no idea that the local news was airing. Todd had walked in just as the lead story, "Double Murders in Frankenmuth," began.

"Well, actually, I wasn't there. Poppy was. She was chasing Munchie and came upon a hand. She was in no danger, and as you just heard, Chief Ed said there is no danger to the public in general."

Todd replied, "Please, take care and stay in well-lit places. Take your phone. Call Ed and then me if anything seems out of line."

Mary Ellen gave Todd a quick kiss, and about three minutes later she pulled into Poppy's driveway. Poppy and Babycakes were in the window, waiting. Poppy walked out shaking her head.

"For goodness sakes, Mary Ellen, put that top up. It's cold, and don't give me the excuse that the heater works. It could snow any day now. Give it up. Top-down season is over."

"Wow, are you in a mood. What's up?"

"These murders are surely connected. Mark's was unexpected. He must have had some damaging information about the killer. That makes me believe that he was involved in the preplanning of Virginia's death," mused Poppy.

"Preplanning, umm. You know, this morning as I was helping Clare clean up, she said she needed to run upstairs to pick up some plates she had left there. She never went upstairs while we were there. She must have been at the Residenz before the van broke down. She was on trip two when we helped her," announced Mary Ellen. "Let's keep an eye on her."

They pulled up to the back of the Residenz, behind Clare's van. They could see that the heat lamps with lights were arranged in a semicircle with chairs spread out around a fire pit. A long table with a blue-and-white checkered cloth was behind the seating. Next to that table was a smaller table with a plain, white cloth that held a large tin bucket filled with ice, beer, and wine. Jim, the bartender, had set up a cart next to that with stronger offerings.

Mary Ellen and Poppy exchanged looks that said, "Here we go again." They walked into the kitchen to find Clare busy unwrapping large aluminum pans. Amazing smells filled the kitchen: barbecue, baked beans, brats, German potato salad, and apple crisp.

"Clare, you have outdone yourself! This is amazing. I'm so glad the Stanleys stepped up and had you do this," said Poppy.

Clare stared at her. "They owe me, and one dinner cannot repay the damage that family has done to me. They are so condescending, just like their horrible Aunt Gin. Ned just wandered down and directed me to make sure that the food was kept warm—really—I needed to be told that?"

Poppy and Mary Ellen were a little taken aback. Clare had been much different in her attitude last night. Maybe they didn't know her that well after all.

"Clare, did Ed or C.J. get to talk to you yet?" asked Mary Ellen. She started arranging condiments on a tray. "Is there brat sauce?"

"Why would they need to talk to me? I was on Main Street with you when the old witch was killed. You are my alibi if I need one." Clare smiled at them. It was not warm and comforting.

Arrabella, Ned's fiancé, walked into the kitchen. She was dressed in leggings and a long satin shirt, not barbecue-friendly clothing. She looked around the kitchen, poking at covered dishes. "Where are the vegetarian items I ordered?" she asked, looking at Clare. Clare glared back at her. "Vegetarian dishes? When did you order them?"

"I called the kitchen this afternoon. My salads should have been delivered." Arrabella looked peeved.

Poppy quickly made a phone call. "Yes, the salads are on the way. Crisis averted."

Mary Ellen took the condiments out to the food table. The twins were already seated by the fire pit. They had brought out more family albums. The light wasn't ideal, so they were using their phone flashlights.

"So what wedding is this?" asked Nelly/Nora. Mary Ellen couldn't tell them apart. Tonight, they wore their hair in braids and had on white shirts and jeans. They were peering at an older picture. Mary Ellen got close enough to see a young, good-looking couple standing in front of a church. The bride's dress looked circa the '60s or '70s.

The girls turned and glared at Mary Ellen. "May we help you? Oh, you're the staff. Can you get us a drink? We'll have a beer—that's a good start for a barbecue."

They turned back to the album. Mary Ellen went to pick up a couple of beers, passing Joe and Amelia as they headed to the fire pit. The twins called to them to sit down and help them figure out who was in the pictures. Nelly/Nora pointed to the wedding picture. "Joe, who is this mystery couple in this wedding picture? Is it Aunt Gin?"

As Mary Ellen gave the twins their beers, Joe raised his hand like he was hailing a cab. "I'll have a bourbon with ice; what brands do you have?"

"The bartender is right over there; you should go talk to him." She wanted to be listening and not serving.

Joe stood up to go to the bar, and over his shoulder said, "Yes, that's Aunt Gin in that photo."

Mary Ellen kept walking to the kitchen. One more little tidbit about the Stanley family.

18: C.J.'S TURN

Put enough people together and you never knew what they could be up to. And it wasn't like none of the locals ever strayed over that line either. As such, C.J. and the chief stuck to their original plan for C.J. to continue doing interviews with the family and anyone else who was at the Residenz the day of the Stanley murder. C.J. had an easygoing way that people tended to let down their defenses around.

Everything about C.J. was carefully planned, including her "nothing to see or fear here" demeanor, which included dressing neither up nor down, her thick brunette hair pulled back in a plain, low ponytail, no jewelry, and light makeup only. She and the chief had worked together for some time. Her ubiquitous outlet-mall jackets hid two firearms, and all her shoes were made for running.

They knew all about the barbecue and decided that arriving around half an hour after it began would be ideal. One might expect that some would have a drink or two under their belts, but they likely weren't over-the-line intoxicated. C.J. could talk to people both alone and in small groups—whatever opportunities presented themselves.

She and the chief planned several lines of questioning, starting with a characterization of their aunt and who benefited from her death. Each person would likely lead the investigation away from themselves. She would be folksy: "We know you all want to help find Virginia's killer; we're all in this together." And she would be firm: "No, you can't leave town yet." This was C.J.'s forte. She did everything short of snagging one of Poppy's lost dogs off the street and bringing it along, and that was mostly because a dog might make someone sneeze, or she'd end up with a mutt like that awful Chuckie and it would be all about him.

She and the chief were on the same page. C.J. left the station and drove to the barbecue in her plain personal vehicle from the local GM dealer in town. For all her calm demeanor and preparation, every nerve tingled with anticipation and the knowledge that she might be face to face with a killer tonight.

19: POINTING THE FINGER

C.J. parked next to Mary Ellen's car in the Residenz parking lot. She noticed Buddy sitting in his patrol car on the side of the road. "Buddy, I see Mary Ellen is here. No Poppy?"

"Oh, they both arrived a little while ago, together."

"Have you ever ticketed that huge van Poppy drives?" asked C.J.

"C.J., you know if we gave a parking ticket to every poor parker in Frankenmuth, we would be out of paper. Remember, we're supposed to be nice."

"But I don't understand how Ed lets those Gladys Kravitz types become part of our business."

Buddy could hear C.J. saying, "Poppy, Puppy, Poopy, I'm coming in," as she walked away.

The family was scattered around the large patio and lawn area, eating appetizers and drinking. "Hi, everyone," she said to pull them together. "And thank you for taking some time to talk to me. These aren't individual interviews, but rather questions where I know the whole group can help our investigation. Kind of a brainstorming session like we have over at the police station, except with the victim's family. There's real value in everyone putting their heads together," she finished. While she was buttering them up, they rearranged themselves so that they could all be seen and heard by each other.

"So," she began, "how would you characterize Virginia? Was she easy to get along with? How close did each of you feel toward her?"

Ned was sitting close to C.J. with his fiancé, Arrabella, who already had a smirk on her face as she listened to the question. But Ned jumped right in with, "Aunt Virginia didn't have an enemy in the world! Look how generous she was bringing us together for this reunion at her own expense. I felt very close to her," he finished as Arrabella actually rolled her eyes. C.J. was making a video recording and was taking in body language and unrecorded signals people might send off, including Arrabella's eyeroll.

Ned's cousin, Joe, cut Ned off with, "Isn't it kind of obvious, Ned, that there's no way we can cover up, shall we say, Virginia's 'difficult' personality characteristics, since someone hated her enough to slit her throat?" Nelly and Nora let out a little gasp at that observation. The twins had a "don't worry, be happy" exterior that cracked easily under pressure. Like now.

Ned was starting to look as huffy as Arrabella and said, "That's a pretty crude reminder of a horrendous thing that happened to poor Aunt Virginia, Joe; thanks for that visual."

Amelia, Joe's wife, came to Joe's defense. "She was a tough old bird. You genuflected almost each time you saw her, like she was the pope, or queen of England. If you weren't obsequious enough, you might find that she sorted your bill separately from the rest and you'd have to pay for your own room as you left," she finished by way of example as to her controlling nature. "Virginia's not just that way with family. She uses money to control any circumstance that she feels the need to control." Amelia's use of the present tense was common this close to a person's death.

One of the twins raised her voice a bit. "Looks like you three have done a great job already, focusing on the family. But there's someone in the kitchen right now," she said, her voice going into a high pitch, "who more than any of us had a motive to kill Aunt Virginia."

C.J. was riveted on this information. "Who might that be? And excuse me, but are you Nelly? Or Nora?"

Nelly/Nora replied, "That Clare woman who is cooking the barbecue. Or whatever she's doing in there!" they echoed, pointing to the kitchen, where Clare was hiding out.

"Well," said C.J., "you all should know better than anyone—aside from the revenge motive you've explained, who benefits from Virginia's death? Let's not focus on who killed her now, but who gets paid. Since you're all here, you can tell me whether, in the event of her death, all of you here would inherit, or one of you, or some of you, or people outside this circle? That doesn't mean you killed her, but it is completely necessary to sort these facts out."

Things got a lot quieter. Joe finally said, "As far as I know, no one knows. The thought is the entire estate stays intact, as it has in the past. While that has previously been the oldest child—not necessarily the son—we aren't on the old Brit system here; it's never been an issue before. Since Aunt Virginia is childless, then it is entirely up to her who benefits. We were told that she wanted to have talks with us all, presumably rethinking her estate planning, but of course, that never happened."

No one disagreed. Every blood relative in the room remained a suspect—Joe, Ned, and the twins. Amelia, Joe's wife, had to be left on the suspect list. But Arrabella was very low or even off the list because Ned had had a lot of fiancés. Tactful as ever, one of the twins used this disappointing information to minimize Arrabella's likely role and Ned nodded in agreement that he couldn't imagine Arrabella thinking she would get paid. While everyone remained a suspect, no one remained a suspect alone since all of them were alibied by each other and those working at the house. While someone might be a conspirator, no one wielded the knife, including Clare, who had Poppy and Mary Ellen as her alibi witnesses.

C.J. popped one final question on them. "What do you think killing the carriage driver, Mark, had to do with all this? Did any of you know him apart from calling the carriage company to arrange a tour for Virginia?"

They all shrugged and denied any knowledge of Mark personally. Ned said, "I wasn't even paying attention to Mark's name, and the only time I communicated with him was when he put Virginia in the carriage and again when they carted her out."

C.J. said, "Thanks, everyone. This has been helpful to put the situation in order. A tech will be here first thing in the morning to take DNA samples from all of you and everyone who worked in this house two days ago."

20: TAKEOUT?

Mary Ellen walked back into the kitchen. Poppy turned toward her and rolled her eyes. Clare was banging dishes and pans around, making more noise than progress at serving food. Mary Ellen glanced to see Clare pouring bags of finely chopped cabbage into a bowl. And sure enough, there were two cartons of a creamy-looking dressing with labels on the top that had been crossed out with a magic marker: Norm's cabbage and coleslaw dressing.

She started to say something when Poppy motioned her over to the counter. Poppy opened the top of an aluminum tray. It was filled with ribs and on the underside of the cover were reheating directions, compliments of Slo' Bones. Both women made eye contact, knowing this food was not prepared by Clare.

The kitchen door flew open, startling everyone. In strode Jim, the bartender, obviously agitated. He headed to the phone on the counter. Poppy asked, "All okay?" He held up a finger and spoke quickly into the phone, then put it down and turned around.

"It seems that the family has upgraded their taste in alcohol. I was here the other night and while Ned, I think his name is, did drink bourbon, now he needs Blanton's. I swear he looked it up online because he called it the good bourbon with the horse on top. I was calling the Lodge to see if they could send up a bottle. They're looking to see what bar might have it. It sure seems like the Stanleys have become fancy."

Mary Ellen laughed, "I didn't think they had been that picky last night. But they enjoyed what they ordered."

Jim laughed, "I was excited to be reassigned up here. They were pretty basic with drinks: wine after they depleted what they brought, beer, a couple of bourbons. The alcohol was here before I set up the cart, so who knows if they helped themselves. Tonight, pretty much the same except for the Blanton's request. I better get outside. If that bourbon shows up, could you bring it outside? Thanks."

Poppy and Mary Ellen went out to set up the Sterno pots. Then they started to bring out the food. Beans and coleslaw from Norm's, Slo' Bones's ribs, Kerns's brats, buns and sauce, German potato salad, and apple crisp that may have been prepared by Clare. The family lined up and generously filled their plates. Clare had come out and was accepting all compliments with a tight smile.

C.J. had joined the family at some point. She was speaking to small groups as they ate. Poppy went over to ask if C.J. would like a plate of food.

"Poppy, oh, and Mary Ellen, you are both here. Of course, you are," C.J. said with a smile. "I'll wait a bit, but a plate of homemade barbecue sounds delicious. This group is clearly enjoying the meal."

"Homemade barbecue is amazing," Poppy replied. She thought she'd save their realizations until she and Mary Ellen could have a good sit-down with C.J. and Ed. C.J. seemed annoyed with their contributions.

After dinner was over and they had cleared up, Clare said, "Thank you so much, ladies. I really needed your help tonight. Next time we meet, coffee is on me. Go and get a good night's sleep. You deserve it." Then she left.

"Well, I guess we have been dismissed," Poppy said. "I certainly didn't expect payment, but I thought more than a cup of coffee was in order. I'll give her the benefit of the doubt; she's as tired as we are. Let's go! And leave the top up."

Mary Ellen got in the car and turned to Poppy. "Benefit of the doubt—she's tired? I'm tired too. You are far nicer than I am. And I'm ordering a large cappuccino when she buys coffee."

The ride home was quiet as both women were thinking about the Stanleys and Clare. When Mary Ellen pulled into Poppy's driveway, she said, "Speaking of coffee, let's meet at the Kaffee Haus early tomorrow and see if we can make some sense out of this."

Poppy nodded. "The Kaffee Haus at half past seven."

Mary Ellen groaned, "Fine; I thought 10:00 was early, but 7:30 it is."

Poppy waved as she hustled to her door. Babycakes was greeting her with welcome barks. The sooner she got to the door, the sooner the barks would stop.

After pulling into her garage, Mary Ellen went into the family room.

"I'm safe and sound. No murders to report. And no leftovers." Leftovers were one of Mary Ellen's favorite things. Todd looked relieved about all three things.

"Welcome home. Grab a wine and relax."

And she did.

21: THE RUG

Mary Ellen got up at seven o'clock knowing she had to be at the Kaffee House at half past. She also knew she would be a few minutes late. She hustled out of the kitchen just in time to meet Todd and announce her coffee date.

"I promise coffee and no murders. I'm going to stop at the library, and I'll be home for lunch."

The Kaffee Haus was a quick drive down Main Street and Mary Ellen arrived only five minutes late. She walked in and spotted Poppy already seated and waving her over.

"I already got your drink."

"You, my friend, are the best. I need a bit of caffeine to clear my head. I feel like we need to rehash the last few days. Two murders that are clearly connected, but how? And that family. They are interesting to say the least. Clare—a coincidence, or not? And Mark—collateral damage or planned? The hand—"

"Slow down." Poppy looked amused. Mary Ellen had a habit of unloading everything that was on her mind in the first five minutes of meeting.

Mary Ellen took a deep breath, a sip of her foamy cappuccino, and sat back in her chair. "I had more to say, but maybe I should slow my roll. I think we need to write down what we know, what we suspect, and what we need to know."

Poppy nodded. "Great idea. Do you have some paper?"

Mary Ellen glanced at her cute little purse. "Nope. But look—it's Tammy and Bri. They'll have paper." She stood and waved. "Girls, do you have any paper we could borrow?"

Tammy waved and nodded. Mary Ellen ran over as Tammy pulled a block of sticky notes out of her backpack. As elementary school teachers, they were never caught without supplies.

"Come join us," said Mary Ellen.

"We can't. We're due at school for a planning meeting. What's new? Did you hear about that lady in the carriage? Good heavens," Bri exclaimed.

Mary Ellen lowered her voice. "Poppy and I were actually there. Let's catch up later. I don't want people to overhear."

Tammy and Bri's eyes widened and both nodded. "This afternoon, a quarter past three, here," said Tammy.

Mary Ellen grabbed the pack of sticky notes. She sat down and Poppy said, "These are too small for all our information."

"Well, one clue per sheet, and we can arrange them on a …" Mary Ellen realized they had to have something to organize them on to make a good visual. She stood up and hurried out the door. Poppy watched as Mary Ellen came back with a mah-jongg rug.

"Um, Mary Ellen. We aren't playing mah-jongg. We're dealing with two murders."

Mary Ellen unrolled the rug with a flourish. "We can put the sticky notes on the rug. It can be rolled up and saved so we can add to our clues or change them."

Poppy gave her two thumbs up. "Let's get to work."

Clues and Facts

Virginia Stanley—victim 1
Wealthy
Drinks gin
Not liked

Mark Thomas—victim 2
Carriage driver
No known connection to Stanley family
Hand cut off, likely drowned, autopsy pending

Joe Stanley
Nephew and oldest relative
In debt
Married to Amelia Stanley

Amelia Stanley
Pain management nurse
Married to Joe Stanley

Elinore and Eleanor Stanley
Identical twins and nieces of Virginia
Visual recognition quirk
Successful financial managers

Ned Stanley
Nephew
Looking for capital to produce play
Engaged to Arrabella, who is looking to star in play

Clare/Maris
Caterer
From same town in Ohio as Stanleys
Virginia smeared her reputation, so she
relocated and in process gave up her dog

The finished product looked pretty spotty, but both women recognized there was more than one suspect in the group. They also realized they had more information from their casual conversations.

Poppy said, "Let's roll it up and each of us take some sticky notes home with us."

So they did, and headed out of the coffee house.

As they walked to their cars, they spied one of the twins with the Col. Sanders guy across the street.

22: MISSING THE MARK

Ed let Poppy occasionally hang out with the cops because she somehow, no matter what the circumstances, knew someone who knew someone who knew the person they needed to know better. The only thing different about today was the coffee house she sat in. She was at the Red Eye, the well-known Old Town Saginaw hangout for cards, poetry, baked goods, and a mean cappuccino, where Poppy had come to meet Sarah.

Sarah was the daughter of an old work colleague of Poppy's and used to work for the carriage company. Since Mark had been with them ten years (very unusual for a driver), there was some overlap. In walked a younger version of Liz, and Poppy waved Sarah over, introducing her and asking what she liked to drink there.

When they were settled with their drinks, Sarah said, "Feel free to ask me anything you want. It's been a few years since I've seen Mark, but he does distinguish himself in ways that are memorable."

"Let's start there then. How so?" asked Poppy.

"I was working partly in the office and partly in the stables back then. One of my jobs was keeping records of employees, especially new ones, up to date. We always did background checks on anyone working or thinking of working there. Our horses were in the drivers' care, not to mention the general public. The city of Frankenmuth expected—actually it was a contractual agreement—that all drivers were cleared of anything relevant to their job to work in the city."

Poppy asked, "Like what? What would be relevant and what wouldn't?"

"Well, pretty much any felony is a deal breaker, and anything that shows a bad temperament, too, even if it's a non-felony thing, would count."

"So, I'm sure the police have looked at his record. I would hope so. Why is it memorable to you?"

"Because it's not there. The record, I mean. We went through all the normal channels while allowing him to go ahead and start working and the record just never came through. And I'll bet on Ace for the win at Churchill Downs, even dragging his buggy, that ten years later, it's still not there."

Poppy asked, "Why would they keep him, and what's your theory of why the record still wouldn't be there or never showed up? What was going on there do you think, Sarah? And why, then, would he still be working there after a decade?"

"I think this guy just doesn't exist on paper, at least not until recently. That's saying a lot in the digital age. I think the guy is just somebody else. Often enough it takes a long time for those records to come in, so it isn't unusual at all for someone to be on the job a while with an incomplete background check. Good buggy drivers are hard to find, and Mark was good at it. He seemed to get along with everyone, including the horses, and he was fun to go to the bar with after work. I think it's as simple as no one wanted to get rid of him. And they didn't. Whoever he was, people in the company never gave any thought to the background check. Including me, honestly. Time flies, and who recalls a good employee having an incomplete background check? No one."

Poppy found that believable.

23: CHECKING IT TWICE

As promised, Mary Ellen met Tammy and Bri back at the coffee house later in the day for their weekly catch-up. Teachers and librarians often knew each other, plus Tammy and Bri were also mah-jongg players. The three had become fast friends.

Friendship or not, Mary Ellen decided to keep the information about the murders brief. So much of what she knew had not been made public knowledge, and it wasn't going to start with her.

The conversation with the girls did make Mary Ellen rethink some of the information on the clue rug. So, first thing the next morning, Mary Ellen grabbed the rug, her mug of coffee, and settled in to take another look at what she and Poppy had put together yesterday.

She realized that she knew more about these people than they had recorded. For example, Virginia had a file of important-looking papers in her room. They needed to know what was in those papers and who had access to them. C.J. had found them, but had someone else taken a look while Virginia was on her carriage ride?

And Mary Ellen recalled that Clare must have had access to the upstairs and all the rooms. She had gone up to collect plates that held sweet treats. Her timeline needed to be tightened up.

It seemed that everybody involved had a motive for wanting Virginia to die. Joe and Ned needed money. Clare had her reputation and business ruined by Virginia. The twins seemed without motive, but they had a habit of making themselves stand out without giving any clues as to what they were thinking. Mary Ellen felt they needed more scrutiny.

Mark's murder was still unexplained, as he had no known relationship to the Stanleys. Poppy was going to find out more about Mark's background. And the hand. The hand seemed like an odd addition to the puzzle. Why cut off a hand?

Mary Ellen heard the back door open. Todd had been running his weekly errands, which included a trip to Kern's for a steak, a stop at Frankenmuth Florist for a bouquet of flowers, and a doughnut from Zehnder's bakery. Mary Ellen got up and poured two cups of coffee.

Todd already had a mouthful of doughnut. He walked over and looked at the rug. "Is this a new version of mahjongg?"

Mary Ellen chuckled and said, "No. It's a clue rug." They had been married long enough for Todd to know that there would be a further explanation. He just had to wait.

Sure enough, Mary Ellen, sounding pleased, said, "We wanted a visual of clues, and the rug was available. This way it's portable and clues can be readjusted and added as information comes up."

Todd frowned. "How involved are you? This is not an Acorn TV show. There have been two murders, M.E. And they have been pretty brutal."

"They have been, and we are bystanders. Chief Ed will ask us for input, as we were technically at each scene. Then we'll sit back and wait for arrests." Todd wasn't all that convinced.

"Well, I might actually have something to add to your board. You know Vida at Frankenmuth Florist? She said a driver actually came in, looked around, and after checking his watch a few times, left. He had the carriage outside at the corner. She thought it was odd, but..."

"What! What day? Would she recognize the driver?" Mary Ellen jumped up, spilling her coffee.

"I didn't ask. I paid and wished her a good day."

"That goes on the clue rug. We may now have a place where Virginia was vulnerable. And now that I think of it, Maisie the cleaning lady thought she saw a carriage stopped. We need to find her and ask her where that happened. Good catch, Todd."

Todd was frowning. "Mary Ellen, do not go asking questions. Bring the rug to Chief Ed and stay away from this investigation."

Mary Ellen was nodding as she added her latest clues to the rug. She couldn't wait to talk to Poppy.

24: THE CYBER DRIVER

Poppy mulled over her new information about Mark, or "Mark," whoever he was. Certainly, from the ages of eighteen through twenty-eight, he'd been Mark. Before that, he was a minor—so what complications would that entail to track him? And would he even be recognizable?

Time for a visit to Facebook world, Twitter, and Instagram. And time to see if Mark could be tracked down.

Poppy was in her house, the one she had shared with her husband up until five years ago when he passed away. Now it was Poppy and the dog, and she was used to it. She came through the door and thought about friends who hoped she'd find someone—but truth be told, she was completely uninterested. She couldn't imagine coming home and some man would also be there who wasn't David. He might want dinner. He might sneeze around her dog. He would no doubt interrupt her thoughts and projects. Mostly, he wouldn't be David. Even going to the movies with a friend was fraught with emotional weight. She thought it was time to just be honest and live her best life instead of making up reasons why no one was suitable for even the most casual of relationships.

She popped open her laptop after feeding Babycakes and pulled up the business Facebook site of the Heritage Carriage Tour Company. Sure enough, there was a page with pictures of all of their drivers who would guide tourists past all the interesting sights in town. And one was labeled Mark Thomas, back when he had both hands and a life.

She did a Facebook search of Mark Thomas and came up with a long list of people with that name. She started hitting each one and eliminated everyone who didn't appear to be in Michigan. She sat there for one long hour doing this and came up with—miracle of miracles—the right Mark. He wasn't big on privacy settings, luckily, which told Poppy he likely wasn't trying hard to hide. She saw an array of friends posting the usual—parties, what was for dinner, all the mundane Facebook stuff.

But then she ran across something she wasn't looking for, which was a good thing sometimes. He posted a couple years ago that he was looking for his "birth father," and he gave information as to when he was born and where. Someone named Stuart wrote back. Then the conversation between the possible father and son went to Messenger, which she couldn't break into.

Holy crap! She was thinking. Did this have anything to do with anything? Could Mark have been killed for reasons completely unrelated to Virginia's death? Had he really met his father, or was the guy a fake hoping to milk something from his "son?"

Mark also—no surprise—had an affinity for animals and posted himself with a variety of horses with dogs hanging out in the background. Poppy couldn't help but do a close-up on the dogs with this guy who had worked years in Frankenmuth. And she let out a second big "holy crap" when she noticed that Munchie was in the background of one of the photos. It was absolutely him—a one-of-a-kind mutt. That cotton picking dog was everywhere but home, thought Poppy.

This struck her as an unrelated coincidence since, indeed, Munchie was everywhere. There were likely thousands of tourists' photos with that dog in the background somewhere. He was friendly and invisible in some ways. Not like mean little Chuckie who everyone would remember, but rather, Munchie was part of the landscape.

Poppy also had Mark's cellphone number. He had a basic and typical iPhone Verizon account, and luckily for Poppy, she had a good friend at the local Verizon store. When Poppy called Hazel and explained—perhaps with a bit of exaggeration as to her actually working for the police on this case—Hazel texted her the last month's phone records on Mark's iPhone. Poppy felt a little guilty hanging up, knowing more than Hazel did that this could be a firing offense, but Poppy wasn't going to directly use these numbers and had no reason to ever disclose Hazel's help. She was just going to use this information to—she hoped—connect to other information.

She started down the list, calling each number. When people picked up, she asked, "Is this the King residence? No? Are you sure? This is the number I have for them and I need to find them—they are my aunt and uncle and I have important family news." Oddly enough, thought Poppy, a lot of them said, "No, I'm sure. This is the Jones residence."

And then there was one other call. A surly male voice answered, "Who is this and where did you get this number?" Poppy hung up. A burner phone, she thought. And an upset person on the other end. At least that was her initial impression of the situation.

Now she had enough to go to Chief Ed to see if his people could make any sense of this and also give him a heads up that this could even be a case unrelated to the Stanley case. That was a reach, but maybe. These child/parent reunions really could go south sometimes. Hard to know why Mark reached out at this point in his life and who he actually connected with.

She slammed the lid on the MacBook and headed on over to first see Mary Ellen and make sure they were on the same page and had the same information.

25: NEEDED: A BIGGER MAH-JONGG RUG

Mary Ellen and Poppy grabbed the bigger table at the coffee shop to spread out their rug with its sticky-note squares.

Poppy started in. "We need a 'Mark' section of the rug—driving the carriage Virginia Stanley died in. Driver around town for ten years without incident. Parked the carriage outside the local florist shop at the time Virginia was in it. Coincidence? Plan? And finally murdered within twenty-four hours of Virginia—another bloody murder, although different (Munchie and the hand, etc.)."

"I take it you've found more news about Mark," said Mary Ellen.

"Yes, although it's more confusing than clarifying."

"Oh, great. Two murdered in town and everyone wants some clarity. The Detroit press have set up shop at the Lodge. They get a free vacation in Frankenmuth. We get news hounds chasing our police around."

Poppy explained the process by which she discovered that Mark might have had two names, but she only found one of them. The social media hunt for his father and a guy popping up who claimed that he was the long-lost dad. And finally, a cranky dude on what might be a burner phone.

"So," Mary Ellen said, "If I'm understanding all this, we have no idea now if Mark's death is or isn't related to Virginia's death."

"Exactly," said Poppy. "It could be a long-lost child moment gone wrong. Or maybe Mr. Dad is connected to both murders, although we've got zero indication of that at the moment. This is where it's time to report to Ed. He's the only one with the resources to figure this out."

"OK," said Mary Ellen. "You go talk to Ed. I'm going to do a little true private-eye work here and shadow a twin. If I can be sure I'm following a twin instead of somehow following both twins. There's something a little odd with the twins."

"You think?" said Poppy. "That whole Stanley clan is pretty weird. OK, let's keep pushing for enlightenment and catch up with each other tomorrow morning. Whatever comes of it or doesn't come of it, we'll learn something."

26: TOX STANDS FOR TOXIC

Poppy headed over to the police station. With two murders having happened in two days, there was an all-hands-on-deck push and no hesitation in using anything available from the state police. Other local police departments were also on alert for anything strange.

The police station/city hall was small, always a balance of up-to-date while not frivolously spending taxpayer money. Everyone was milling around the assembly room where extra folding chairs had been set up. Poppy went around making small talk until she could get hold of the chief, who, she was told, would be there soon. In true small-town form, these officers were friends and neighbors on the whole. Sandi said to her, "Wow, I heard Munchie dropped the second case right on your face!" A couple people, including Poppy, chuckled, although Poppy still wasn't chuckling on the inside about that.

Chief Ed walked into the room and everyone grabbed a seat, including Poppy, who sat near the back trying to be inconspicuous. She figured this was as good a time as any to catch up on what the police had discovered.

C.J. looked over and spotted the interloper right away but before she could suggest that Poppy ... well ... get out, the chief started the meeting and clearly didn't want anything slowing him down.

"The tox report on Virginia Stanley came in from the state police just now and we do have some interesting information from it. Anything that can help us think this through is important. And we need to stop the literal bleeding in this town."

He had their attention.

"Virginia had a small array of usual prescription drugs in the normal amounts in her system for a woman of her age. Nothing alarming. What is alarming, considering the fact she had her throat cut as the proximate cause of death, is that she also had a considerable overdose of zolpidem in her system."

This caused a stir in the room.

Every full- or part-time police officer in town was a fully certified EMT, so they all knew that Virginia had what amounted to enough Ambien in her system to cause her to sleep on her carriage tour. Not for the first time did Poppy think about Mark driving around giving his spiel about the local businesses and sights to either an unconscious or dead Virginia. The whole thing was getting weirder, if that was even possible.

Poppy was able to sit down with Ed for a few minutes after the meeting. Ed, for his part, was equally creeped out about how this was all going and interested in seeing if Poppy and Mary Ellen had discovered anything.

Poppy took Ed through her excursion into social media after explaining that Mark's background report never came back from the company which ran that, for whatever reason. "At first I thought maybe Mark wasn't Mark but someone else entirely, and that's why the carriage company doesn't have a background report on file. That the whole thing just got forgotten considering that they needed drivers and he was doing a good job with both the horses and the customers.

"But he doesn't appear to be someone else. Instead, he was trying to find out his own background by searching for his father. And it appears he had found him."

Poppy pulled up her laptop and showed Ed the threads about the dad search up to the point Mark and his reputed father left the public sphere to presumably set up a meeting in a more private setting. She finished the whole story about Facebook and Verizon and even a possible burner phone, leaving Ed with the same question Poppy had. Did any of this have anything to do with Virginia's murder, or was it a coincidental thing that after decades and decades of no murders in Frankenmuth, they now had two unrelated ones? While he had to consider it, all of his instincts, including that Virginia died in Mark's carriage, told him no—these killings had to be related.

He needed to track this down.

27: PRINTS AND SWABS

C.J. made a call to Judy and asked that any staff who had been at the Residenz during the day and evening of Virginia Stanley's arrival meet in the dining room. She then placed a call to Clare, the caterer. Clare was less than thrilled to hear from C.J. but agreed to attend.

C.J. had called the Bridgeport office of the state police and asked that a fingerprint technician meet her at the Residenz. When she pulled into the driveway, she was glad to see a state police official car already there. And right behind it ... Mary Ellen's convertible. C.J. was annoyed that at least one of the private eyes was there. But she also realized that Mary Ellen was on the scene when Virginia's body was found. Grumbling to herself, she walked up to the front door and knocked.

Joe answered the door. "We've gathered in the dining room. Quite a crowd." C.J. followed him inside.

"Good morning. I'm Officer Thompson. My colleague, Officer Baker, is upstairs collecting prints from the deceased's bedroom. Joe was kind enough to point us in the correct direction."

C.J. shook the officer's hand. She turned and looked at Joe. "How did you get into Virginia's room?"

Joe shrugged. "Her key has been on the table with all the other keys. She must not have taken it with her."

C.J. looked around the table to make sure all the people she needed were available. "Where is Arrabella?"

Ned sighed, "She broke a nail and is fixing it. She'll be right down."

C.J. said, "I'll do DNA swabs and Officer Thompson will do fingerprints. I'd like to do the Lodge staff first so they can get back to work. This shouldn't take too long."

Amelia cleared her throat. "Why do we need to have our fingerprints and DNA taken? Are we suspects? Do we need a lawyer?"

C.J. stopped arranging her swabs and containers. "The toxicology report on Virginia Stanley shows she had zolpidem in her system, enough to sedate her. We don't know if she took it herself or if it was given to her. These tests should rule out innocent people. Mark, the carriage driver, had material under his nails. The DNA test will likewise rule out the innocent. As to an attorney, you are welcome to call one. He can meet us at the police station and watch us administer the test to you."

Amelia looked at Joe. He whispered that since they had nothing to do with either murder, they should cooperate. Amelia looked a little concerned but nodded.

With both C.J. and Officer Thompson working together, the group was done in no time. The officer who was in charge of dusting Virginia's room for fingerprints came down and the three law enforcement officers left together.

The Lodge staff and Clare left as soon as they were finished. Mary Ellen, after moving her car so the police could leave, had walked back in. The twins, both with phones in hand, were seated in the living room.

"So, do you think your aunt took sleeping medication?" Nelly/Nora looked up. "Sorry, we were doing some work." She nudged her sister. "Did you want something?"

"I was just wondering if your aunt took sleeping medication?"

The twins shook their heads. "Is that what that stuff is? We really didn't know her well enough to learn her habits. Ask Amelia; she might know. She's a nurse."

With that, they both put their ear buds back in and started scrolling on their phones.

Mary Ellen went into the dining room. She could hear voices in the kitchen. She heard Joe say, "Why are you worried? You had nothing to do with Aunt Gin's death."

Amelia sounded scared. "My fingerprints will be in that room and I'm a nurse. I know about drugs."

Mary Ellen decided to quietly leave through the front door. She needed to talk to Poppy.

28: BARNEY

Poppy thought a lot about the questions from the press appearance that the reporters had asked. And she thought some more about the information she was privy to now, the tox report having shed more light on how someone could have killed Virginia in that carriage. Who could get close enough to Virginia to drug her, as well as get close enough to kill her in the carriage? More and more she was also leaning toward a possible conspiracy to kill Virginia.

Did Mark in fact kill her in his own buggy, and then the person who sedated her killed Mark to dispose of that connection? Was Mark desperate enough for money to actually commit murder? It seemed uncharacteristic of what she could dig up about his history. Although he might have wanted to move on, generally he liked the horses, and the job was easy enough as long as you could schmooze with tourists—and Mark definitely had that sort of personality.

Poppy was sipping a short glass of dry white as she kicked these ideas around. Babycakes sat on her lap making snuffling noises as Poppy stroked her brindle coat and rubbed her neck. Babycakes helped her think. It was pretty meditative hanging out with a dog.

Her phone came alive with a barking ring, which Babycakes knew better than to make a fool out of herself about. Babycakes had learned to ignore it—for some odd reason, she knew there was no actual dog behind that bark.

Poppy didn't recognize the number but decided to answer it anyway—in her line of work, such as it was, you never knew.

"Hello?"

"Uh, hello, Poppy? This is Poppy, right?"

"Yes. Barney? Is that you?"

"Yes! From Ohio—you might recall that's where I practice law now."

"I do recall that," said Poppy, and added, "although I never did quite get why, if you were leaving Michigan, you'd only get as far as Ohio."

"Yes, well, that's one of those questions that I just don't have an answer to. Haha."

Poppy was considering the discomfort Barney always had with small talk as she listened to his forced chuckle and awaited the purpose of the call, which certainly wasn't to catch up with Poppy.

Professional Barney kicked in. "Well, I'm sure you're wondering why I'm calling. And I'm getting to that. But I really do hope you've been doing OK since David died. I think that's been, what, five years? And we haven't talked since the funeral."

"I'm doing OK, Barney, really. It's nice to hear from you—but what's up?"

"I need to come to Frankenmuth and thought you could give me the lay of the land up there in Murder City," Barney responded. He added, "I've never been there."

"What? How is it your office was thirty minutes away in Flint for years and you never had a chicken dinner in Frankenmuth?" Poppy really was surprised on the one hand but considering how intensely Barney worked, it made sense he wasn't running thirty minutes up the road to have lunch.

"Well, I'm going to fix that now. Of course, I know you'll understand that I'm asking you for information but cannot give you a lot of information in return."

She rolled her eyes. Indeed, she did know that. Barney Mead and David had practiced law out of the same building for a while—not in association with one another but as separate renters of space in a building full of lawyers. The two of them hit it off, having complementary eccentricities and work ethics. Oh, and quirky senses of humor. Barney was a good twenty years younger, and at the time at the start of a stellar and unusually eclectic career.

"How can I help? And how can you possibly have any connection to these murders?" she asked.

"Well, I can tell you just a little about that. This will be publicly filed information so I can tell you that I helped Virginia Stanley with her estate planning, and, while I don't normally encourage clients to do this, I agreed in this case to be named as personal representative of her estate to carry out her wishes as to the disposition of her property in the event of her death. And here we are."

"No kidding! So, what are her wishes as to the 'disposition of her property in the event of her death,' Barney?"

"Well, I can't tell you that just now. But I'm hoping you can advise me where to stay. Apparently, there's some kind of festival up there. So far, I haven't been able to find a room. And if you're still doing investigative work, I'd like to hire you—someone I can trust—and then confidentiality will attach to you also and we can talk about this a whole lot more."

"I have a partner in the investigative biz," Poppy said, and mentioned Mary Ellen. "And full disclosure, I spend a lot of my time chasing lost dogs. Not murder investigations."

"OK, the Stanley estate can afford two investigators. I need someone to help me navigate the, let's say, culture and crosscurrents of the town."

"Barney, I have three spare bedrooms here. You're welcome to one of them gratis, as you would always have been welcome here. The three of us can put together what we all—all three of us," she emphasized, "might know or surmise. But make it soon. These murders need to be solved soon."

"You think they are related?"

"I do. But I don't know that yet."

"I'll be there tomorrow. Please arrange a time where I can talk to both you and … Mary Ellen," he said, tripping just a little over Mary Ellen's name.

"And thanks for the room. I'll take it."

"Great," Poppy said. I have a dog named Babycakes. You aren't nervous around dogs, are you? She's very sensitive."

"I'm pretty sensitive myself," quipped Barney. "We'll get along fine."

●●●

Poppy hung up and called Mary Ellen. No sooner did they get done talking than the doorbell rang and, as always, Babycakes tried to answer it. Poppy opened the door and found Clare standing there with a covered paper plate in her hand. Poppy was thinking she could use a goodie from a good caterer right now—perhaps that was part of the thank you for helping Clare out.

Clare had leaned down to gush over Babycakes, who obliged by rolling over for a belly rub. "Oh, you are such a cutie!" Clare said. "And I brought you some special dog treats that I used to bake for my own pup."

Her voiced trembled a tiny bit, Poppy noticed. But sure enough, she had homemade dog treats. Without asking, she gave Babycakes one of the treats and it disappeared immediately. Poppy reached over and gently took the treats from Clare, thanking her, and putting them in the kitchen for later.

When the treats disappeared, so did Babycakes. "Unusual," Poppy thought.

"I just thought your dog might enjoy those. They are healthy and feature pumpkin."

"Thanks," Poppy said.

"And it gave me a chance to meet the famous Babycakes, too. If you ever need someone to walk her because you're caught up in a long day of work, do give me a call. Maybe dog walking is a little side business I could cultivate."

"That might work," Poppy said.

Babycakes didn't reappear until Clare left. "Where have you been?" Poppy asked the dog. "It's time to get ready for bed." Babycakes trotted ahead to the bedroom, always ready for a good night's sleep.

29: THE POLICE MEET THE GLUE RUG

Mary Ellen and Poppy met in front of the police station. They thought it was a good time to share some of the thoughts they had with Chief Ed and C.J. Mary Ellen had the mahjongg rug rolled up and stored in a drawstring bag.

"I'm not sure this rug is going to be well received. It might be a little quirky for police brains," said Mary Ellen. "It helps me keep all the players straight, but Ed and C.J. may not appreciate our method."

Poppy looked at Mary Ellen. "It's our style. Let's roll it out."

The two friends walked in and were directed to the chief's office.

Ed greeted them with a questioning smile. "Ladies, may I help you?"

Poppy and Mary Ellen smiled back. Mary Ellen said, "We think we may have some information that might help with the murders. Because we have been up at the Residenz and around town, we may have heard and seen some items of interest."

C.J. appeared at the door. Ed said, "Come on in, C.J. I was just about to call you. The ladies have some information for us. Mary Ellen, Poppy, have a seat."

Poppy looked around the office. "Can we go to the conference room? The rug will need to be spread out."

C.J. looked annoyed. "The rug? We have got to get cracking on those forensic reports and schedule more interviews."

Chief Ed looked over at Mary Ellen and Poppy, then back at C.J. "I think we need to see what they have. Let's take a look."

C.J. rolled her eyes and led the way, followed by Mary Ellen, Poppy, and Ed. Mary Ellen pulled out her mah-jongg rug and unrolled it on the long table. Ed and C.J. leaned in for a better look.

Ed straightened up and looked at C.J. "This is interesting. I see how relationships are shown."

C.J. nodded. "This is helpful. Is there new information on here that we don't have?"

Mary Ellen said, "I'm not sure what you have versus what we have. The two newest pieces involve the carriage ride and Clare, the caterer."

Ed looked up at Mary Ellen. "What about the carriage ride?"

"It seems that Mark stopped the carriage and went into the Frankenmuth Florist. Todd was there today, and Vida mentioned that a carriage had stopped there, and the driver had stood around, looked at his watch, and left. Todd didn't ask what day this happened, but a visit to the florist might be in line. Plus, we heard Maisie (the one with the house cleaning service), mention a stopped carriage by the florist. She might remember the day because of her cleaning schedule."

C.J. was scribbling on her notepad. "We knew the carriage had to have stopped somewhere."

Ed asked, "What's the other clue you have?"

"Well, the morning after Virginia was found, I went back up to the Residenz to help Clare pack everything up. At the very last minute, Clare said she had to run upstairs and grab some dishes she had left up there. Poppy and I never saw her go upstairs the night before. She must have been at the Residenz before her van broke down," Mary Ellen replied.

Ed looked at C.J. thoughtfully. "So, Clare had access to the rooms upstairs before the carriage ride. That puts her firmly on the suspect list. Pick her up tomorrow and bring her in for questioning. C.J., you get with Vida and Maisie. We'll meet back here and compare notes."

Ed turned to Poppy and Mary Ellen. "Thank you for your help. I'm going to take a picture of your clue rug. Is there a better word for it? Let us know what else you come across."

With that said, both officers quickly left the room. Mary Ellen rolled up her rug and she and Poppy left the police station.

As they stood by their cars, Poppy said, "That went really well. I think we have almost been deputized."

Mary Ellen rolled her eyes. "Let's meet tomorrow and see where we go next. After lunch works best for me; I have some mah-jongg to play in the morning."

30: ED TALKS TO CLARE

As planned, C.J. approached the coffee shop from the back of the parking lot, quickly spotting Poppy's "mini" van, taking up one whole space and enough of a second to render it unusable to anyone in a vehicle with a motor.

C.J., while forever and always irritable about Poppy's parking (which clearly, C.J. thought, showed a lack of regard for law and order, or at least order) was beginning to see how this choreographed pick up of a suspect was a true time-saver and smacked of a rather nifty piece of theater.

The detective was driving a big Frankenmuth Police SUV. As she approached the coffee house, she turned on every light and gave the siren a bit of a "wrrrp, wrrrp" sound as she pulled "a Poppy" and parked at a crooked angle very close to Clare and Poppy's table. She considered this effective policing, of course. Poppy for her part very much admired the maneuver.

While Poppy remained silent, C.J. approached the table—ignoring Poppy—and zeroed in on Clare. "I'm going to have to ask you to come with me, Clare. The chief needs to talk to you at the station." Poppy waited for Clare to say, "Not without my lawyer," or "No thanks, maybe later." Instead, Clare stood up and headed toward the cruiser.

Poppy not for the first time wondered how much she and Mary Ellen could get done with this imprimatur of officialdom attached to one of their vehicles. C.J. opened the back door and Clare climbed in behind the wire cage separating the front seat from the back. With a slight nod of acknowledgement to Poppy, C.J. hopped in the driver's seat and took off, heading the few blocks over to the police station.

Clare was escorted to the station's one and only interview room and told the chief would join her soon. Thirty minutes later, Ed entered, all business with a report in his hand.

"Clare Kincaid, you are not under arrest, but you are being questioned about the possibility of your role in the murder of Virginia Stanley." He went on to assure her of what her rights were, including the right to a lawyer. She said she understood and didn't ask to call a lawyer. This was one of life's most surprising things to Ed. Why would anyone under these circumstances agree to talk to him at all, let alone without a lawyer? Yet, people mostly did. It's like they were afraid asking for a lawyer would be evidence of guilt. But as Ed saw it, by the time they were sitting where Clare was, someone was somewhat convinced they'd done something wrong anyway.

Ed explained in plain language the toxicology evidence found in Virginia's body, which would have at the very least rendered Virginia groggy during the carriage tour. Before he could get to the part about DNA found underneath Virginia's fingernails, Clare shocked him by sobbing out a confession right on the spot.

"Yes, I did drug her! I did! I'm so sorry. She was so mean to me in the past. I just didn't want her to enjoy the carriage ride. Instead, people would assume she was just a passing-out drunk old lady! Those people act like they own the place. I hated that she came to the town where I moved."

As the camera rolled from its perch outside the room, Ed paused for a moment to take this in. He knew she didn't personally kill Virginia. Her whereabouts away from the carriage route were accounted for by many people. But did she have a partner who killed Virginia out of revenge for Clare's past humiliations with the Stanley clan? Was it really Mark? Did Clare kill Mark and then, finding herself semi-arrested, crack under the pressure? Would she admit to that next?

Ed said, "We found some DNA under Virginia's fingernails. Male DNA. How about you get this whole thing off your conscience and tell us who your partner was in planning to kill Mrs. Stanley?"

"What?" shouted Clare. "No, I didn't kill her, and I don't know who did. I didn't have a partner at all. I just had an opportunity to make her sleep through her carriage ride. That's it. That's all. I want a lawyer!"

Well, thought Ed, that could have gone better. On the other hand, it went a lot better than he really thought it would—Clare having confessed to a critical part in Virginia's murder.

"Clare Kincaid, you're under arrest for assaulting Virginia Stanley. Other charges may be pending soon. Legal counsel of your choice may be called, or we will find someone for you. And you will be transferred to the county jail as soon as we can process you in."

Ed exited the interview room and said to C.J., "Whew. At least we have someone sitting in jail who confessed to something here. That's got to be progress."

31: THE GUY WITH POPPY

The next morning, Mary Ellen grabbed her first cup of coffee and her phone and settled in her favorite chair. Todd was already checking his emails and news apps. Mary Ellen sent a quick mah-jongg invite to a few friends. She desperately needed a mah-jongg fix.

"So, have you handed over all your clues to Chief Ed?" asked Todd, peering at Mary Ellen over his glasses.

"Yes, and today I am playing mah-jongg, making a list of things to do before the holidays, and maybe even taking a little nap. Life is back to normal," answered Mary Ellen. She finished her coffee and collected her bag of tiles, a non-clue rug, and her purse.

"See you later. If you need me, I'm at the Kaffee Haus and I have my phone with me." With that said, Mary Ellen got into her car and headed to town. It was a typical late fall day, a little dreary, but no rain or snow.

The parking lot at the Kaffee Haus was almost empty, so Mary Ellen parked close to the door. As she stepped out of her car, Pat M. pulled into the space next to her, with Sharon B. in the passenger seat. Mary Ellen was thrilled to see them both. They were both fun and good players. As they walked in, Mary Ellen noticed Mary C. already seated. This would be a good mah-jongg morning.

Mary Ellen called out her cappuccino order and went up to start setting up the tiles. "Good morning."

"Good morning to you. Let me help you with those tiles," said Mary C.

After everyone had their coffee and was seated, they started to build their walls. Pat M. cleared her throat. "So who's the guy at Poppy's house?"

Sharon B. looked at Mary Ellen. "The one who was walking Babycakes this morning. Early."

Before Mary Ellen could answer, Mary C. said, "Oh, another mystery. So, who is this guy? Nice looking? Mary Ellen? Spill."

Mary Ellen looked around at the friends. Sharon and Pat were neighbors of Poppy's, so of course they would know of visitors, especially male visitors.

"He's a long-time friend of Poppy and David's. He's an attorney who has business in Frankenmuth. Poppy, of course, invited him to stay with her. It's so much nicer than a long stay in a hotel room."

"A long stay?" asked Sharon. They were waiting for Mary C. to discard a tile and start the game.

"Well, at least until his business is finished. This is a strictly platonic relationship. They have known each other a long time and you know Poppy—once a friend, always a friend. Mary, are you going to discard?"

"West wind, hopefully we'll get to meet this guy."

Just then Mary Ellen's phone dinged. She looked down. A message from Poppy: "Drop by this morning when you can."

32: BARNEY STRIKES A DEAL

Barney had taken Poppy up on her invitation and moved into a spare bedroom. He also used another one that had a small desk as an office. Poppy thought that he looked like he might be there a while. She was fixing herself a cup of coffee. Barney declined and kept working. Mary Ellen would be over in a few minutes for a business meeting among the three of them.

Barney emerged from his office to joyous leaps from Babycakes, who would absolutely be fine greeting him with like-new enthusiasm fifty times a day if that was what hospitality required of her—and she hoped it was.

It was hard for Poppy to imagine that Barney had time in his life for a dog (after all, she thought, he didn't manage to find time in his life for the succession of wives who had moved on), but he made a fair effort at appreciating Babycakes's rollovers, high fives, twirls, sits (right in his path, but impressive sitting), and back-leg, tall-girl dancing to make herself more obvious, and, as Poppy figured it, taller and harder to miss as Babycakes walked him toward the treat bowl on the counter.

Barney, though, had just noticed that there was a mah-jongg set, tiles, racks, and pushers on a mat set up on the kitchen table. "Oh, you play mah-jongg?" he asked Poppy, and without waiting for a response, he went on, "My nana played mah-jongg with her friends, and she taught me to play. I still have her old set. Yellow antique tiles, no jokers, but plenty of flowers to sticker, a family heirloom for sure."

"Wow," said Poppy. "I never imagined you playing games like this."

"Oh, I love the strategy of it," he said. "It's a great game. And there's this maven over in New Jersey, her name's Bubbe Fischer, and you know what she says about strategy?"

Barney was about to tell her, but this wasn't news to Poppy. They both together said, "If you can't win, don't lose!" And laughed.

"I love the game for sure," said Poppy, "but our local maven is Mary Ellen."

As if on cue, there was a light knock at the door. Babycakes was all over it, barking and leaping and looking out the front window at Mary Ellen waving to her.

When they got settled and introductions were made, Barney took charge of the conversation.

"Listen," he said, "I guess you two work as a team. And that's great because I need a team, I think, to do some local investigative work as well as to think all this through with me. So, we need to make this official or I can't talk to you about information that I have that's relevant, possibly relevant to Virginia's murder; I don't know yet."

Barney, old friends with Poppy and her husband David, quickly won over Mary Ellen. He was very persuasive. They came up with an hourly rate and some minimal expectations of what the job would entail, and just like that, Barney had a two-page contract with all their signatures on it.

"Barney, can you now tell us something about the estate planning that Virginia had done or was thinking of doing? It did occur to everyone that this murder wasn't random, so the police are certainly trying to figure out who had a motive."

Barney took a breath, sighed, and started in. "This is quite a story," he began, and kept going. "The usual estate planning protocols really were tossed out the window for the most part. I'm sure you think what everyone involved thinks—that Virginia was a childless elderly lady who has a collection of nieces and nephews, none of whom she's especially close to but who genuflect a couple times a year, trying their best not to be cut out of her will as logical heirs."

Barney looked at Poppy. "Do you have a bottle of water or glass of water that I could have?" Poppy fetched water for all three of them, and Barney continued.

"Virginia does have an ex-husband roaming around somewhere, and we can talk about him later because before this latest incarnation of her estate planning, she had never cut him out. It's possible if he hears of her death, he may show up and expect to inherit. I sure would consider that a long reach since they haven't been in touch in decades. But it's part of the mix in her story. We are under no obligation to notify him."

He gurgled down half the bottle of water. "Because of her age, Virginia has kept certain information to herself. That's why she came to see me—to see what to do with this information now."

Poppy and Mary Ellen raised an eyebrow at one another, then at Barney. This really was getting interesting.

"Virginia had a high school sweetheart back when she was in the tenth grade. Long story short, she got pregnant, he walked away from her, and her parents sent her to a convent that specialized in such situations, where she gave birth to a live, healthy child—this much she was told—and she never knew if she had a son or daughter."

There was an audible gasp from Poppy and Mary Ellen at once. Sensing opportunity, Babycakes leaped into Barney's lap, holding a small stuffed chipmunk with the stuffing removed from his head. Understanding the expectation, Barney tossed the chipmunk over the back of the couch and Babycakes took off after it.

He continued. "That's how some of these places did things back then. She was required to sign adoption papers up front and other than acknowledging that she gave birth to a healthy baby, she never saw the child or was given any information. She went back to school next fall, and there were rumors, but these were discreet times, and Virginia graduated on time and went on to a university education. The father of her child felt that he dodged a bullet and had no interest. No one cared back then anyway, and he wasn't required to sign anything."

Mary Ellen interjected, "That child is how old now? That child is a legal heir?"

"Well, you make a great point, Mary Ellen. Normally, the child would have absolutely no rights to any part of Virginia's estate. But in this case," he continued, pulling out a pile of papers from his briefcase, "Virginia had me draw up a trust document, which she duly executed, that favored this missing child to the tune of receiving one hundred percent of her estate. All these nieces and nephews around her were cut right out. If any of them murdered her to inherit, they'll be in for a shock. In addition to prison, they wouldn't get a cent for their trouble."

"Wow! Chief Ed will want to hear about this."

"I'm sure he will and I'm glad to share it with him to try to see if that helps us track down my client's killer. But meantime, I need you both with your contacts and your investigative skills to please do your best to track down the missing child of Virginia Stanley."

They both quickly agreed they were in. Poppy thought she could only round up Munchie and Chuckie so many times without wishing to find something a little harder to predict, and where she didn't need to dumpster dive at Subway for bait.

They played a couple games of three-person mah-jongg. The girls got beaten by the lawyer who hadn't played in thirty years. No one was surprised.

33: SISTERS OF MERCY

Poppy arrived at the Red Eye Café early. She glanced next door at Old Town Tattoo, wondering if getting another tattoo might be a great idea. But no time today.

Father Bob of Frankenmuth's Catholic Church was a friend of Poppy's and had even come out of retirement for David's funeral five years ago. Occasionally she liked to buy him a cup of coffee and often Mary Ellen joined them. Mary Ellen was busy doing other investigative work, so it was just Poppy today.

She was nervous because she wasn't sure where the boundaries were for giving her information when it came to nuns and adoptions—how confidential was all that? But she was sure he'd be sure and set her straight either way.

He strolled in, happy to see a cappuccino awaiting him. He was dressed in jeans, gardening work shoes, and a casual shirt. Gardening was a passion for him and golfing a social pleasure. He and Poppy shared a love of fiction, normally mystery/thriller-type genres. They had both recently read the new book by Erik Larson, a favorite nonfiction writer who had written his first work of fiction. *No One Goes Alone* was only on audiobook because, Larson said, "All ghost stories are better told." They spent some time discussing the concepts of ghosts and evil incarnate and whether those could be the same thing—and if so, where did it reside? What could it do? Did it live on in perpetuity? Larson speculated on all that and Poppy and Father Bob added their own speculations to the conversation.

Then Poppy shifted into business. "Mary Ellen and I are investigating a case—we were actually hired by this Ohio lawyer, and it's related to the murders in town," she explained.

"Oh!" said Father Bob. "Is that the guy staying at your house who is seen walking Babycakes early in the morning?" he asked with a gleam in this eye.

They both burst out laughing. "Rumors already?" asked Poppy.

"Small town living," answered Father Bob.

"He was having trouble finding a place to stay," she added.

"Ah. One festival after another this time of year."

They both said at the same time, "And every time of year."

"He's around twenty years my junior and a mutual friend of mine and David's."

"So now I'm curious what I can add to unraveling this case," he said.

"Well, I'm going to fall on your good graces and expertise at keeping confidences," she said. Poppy told him a little about Virginia Stanley, a lot of which was now public, but then she added the information that wasn't public as of yet. "Virginia had a child out of wedlock when she was sixteen and in high school. One of those boyfriend things that got out of hand. She was seventy-one when she was killed, and this child would be around fifty-five now. Virginia delivered him or her—she was never told—in a convent around northwest Ohio that long ago. This child stands to inherit a sizeable fortune but records just are harder to come by than they might be now. No computers back then. Nuns coming and going. Children given in casual adoptions. We don't know where to begin to trace her. Or him. It's definitely to this middle-aged person's advantage to be found at the moment. Where would you suggest I begin?"

"You're right—sometimes these records just aren't kept very well, or you might get lucky. The only convent that exists now and was doing that kind of work then in northwest Ohio is Our Sisters of Mercy, just south of Findley."

"Do they still take in mothers and babies and do adoptions?"

"Oh, no. Last I heard the Sisters of Mercy convent is a retirement home these days for a few of the older nuns who just need to live out their lives in peaceful contemplation."

"What are the odds that someone is there now who was there then and will talk to me?"

"Long," answered the priest. "But it's your only option— take a drive down there and see what you and Mary Ellen can find out. If you convince one knowledgeable nun there that there's no one who can be harmed by this information now but only helped, you could get lucky and that's the approach you ought to take. Not to mention, one of their girls from so long ago getting murdered ought to offend them."

Poppy pulled out her phone and located what she thought was likely the old convent on her Google maps. "What do you think?" she asked. "Is this the place?"

"I believe so."

"Thank you! This does help. At least we have a starting point and have to hope someone will remember the situation."

They wandered out to their cars, discussing his latest golf trip and parting ways until the next time.

34: MARY ELLEN EXPLAINS "PAPERCHASE" TO TODD

Mary Ellen left Poppy, knowing she had to go home and explain to Todd that she might be involved, or still be involved, in the Stanley case. Todd was very supportive of all Mary Ellen's activities. The problem was this activity involved murder, actually two murders, and Todd was worried about her safety. She pulled into the garage and steeled herself for a "discussion."

"Hey, you're home! I was just going to make some lunch. What do you feel like?" Todd welcomed her.

"Well, how about a talk. Let's go sit down." She flashed her most winning smile.

Todd, who knew that smile, said, "We don't need to sit down. Grab a stool and spill the beans, my sweet."

Mary Ellen hugged her guy and sat at the island. "So, I went to Poppy's, and her friend, Barney Mead, was there. It turns out he was Virginia Stanley's attorney. Her will was going to be shared with the family, but there's a glitch. None of them is a beneficiary. She had a child out of wedlock in her teens who will inherit. At this point, the identity of this child is unknown—oh, by the way, this isn't for anyone's ears but yours. Anyway, Barney asked Poppy and me to do a little investigating for him."

Todd looked at his still-smiling wife. "And … I know you, Mary Ellen, this is more than a little investigating."

"Well, I signed a contract because we get paid. How cool is that?"

"You signed a contract to find the missing heir of a murdered woman whose first contact in Frankenmuth is a carriage driver who has also been murdered? Do I have that correct?"

"Todd, it's going to be a paper chase. The child was adopted. We will be digging through a mountain of legal documents. Listen, I need to text Poppy and meet up with her. We'll talk more at dinner." With that, Mary Ellen hopped off her stool and headed for the garage.

●●●

Once in the car, Mary Ellen texted her friend, "Heading to T-Dubs for lunch. Join me so we can catch up."

Almost immediately, a reply: "Just back in town. See you there. Lots to share."

The two women met in the T-Dubs parking lot. "Excellent timing," they both said.

Poppy was bubbling with information. "Let's sit down, and I'll fill you in."

They grabbed a seat and started to talk. But Poppy looked around and nudged Mary Ellen. "Isn't that the Stanley family?"

Sure enough, front and center in the big window looking out on the downtown sidewalk was the entire Stanley clan. They had just ordered food and were sipping drinks.

Ned looked down the table at Joe. "So, you think Gin left the whole pile to you? Sure would solve a lot of problems if you had an inheritance. Although, you know, you can't murder someone and benefit."

Joe pushed back his chair and glared at Ned. "I did not kill Gin, and you know it. You're hoping she left you something for your 'Fine Arts,' whatever that is. And you had as much opportunity as I did."

Poppy looked at Mary Ellen. "Things do not seem idyllic in Stanleyland."

Nelly/Nora waved their hands. "Stop this now. We don't know what's in the will and until we do, let's not point fingers." She looked around. "And let's not cause a scene in a public place, bringing attention to ourselves."

Mary Ellen looked at Poppy. "We saw that guy, the Colonel Sanders guy, the other day. And I saw him again with one of the twins. He needs a good look over."

The Stanleys' food arrived, stopping all conversation as they dug into the apparently excellent lunch.

Poppy pulled a notebook out of her purse. "Let me tell you about all the looking we need to do. Let's share a pizza and get to work."

With that, Poppy filled Mary Ellen in on Father Bob's information and they proceeded to make a plan. After both ate two pieces, they mapped out their strategy. Poppy grabbed the takeout box and stood up.

"I'll take this to Barney. He must be starving. I'll let him know that we will be starting our investigation with a trip to Ohio. I'll check with you in the morning. Can Todd get us a hotel room in case we need it? He'll know where we should stay."

Mary Ellen gathered her purse and phone. "Sure, travel reservations are right up his alley. I'll put him on that and text you the info. See you tomorrow." The girls walked out together.

•••

Instead of following Mary Ellen up Main Street, Poppy took a detour. She turned onto Tuscola, then up Cherry Street. As she turned onto Genesee Street, she saw her friend Gil at his appointed corner. Gil was a longtime crossing guard for the Frankenmuth school district, following his retirement from the local sheriff's department. He was famous for his high fives with the elementary kids, and warm greetings. He knew every kid's birthday and presented them with treats to celebrate. They all loved Mr. Gil.

Poppy got to know Gil and become friends with him after he pointed her in the right direction of Munchie on several occasions. Poppy pulled over, rolled down the window, and greeted Gil with a good question. "Gil, how are you? Is that a hand hanging out of your pocket?"

Gil grinned and pulled out a bloody rubber stump from his pocket. "Hello, Poppy. Took this from some middle-school boys who were torturing some middle-school girls by waving it around. That murder has captured all their imaginations. I'll run it over to the school. They can handle it. Haha! So, are you looking for Munchie? He hasn't been around."

Poppy laughed at the hand and Gil's joke. "No, just stopped to say hi. You don't know anything about that murder, do you?"

"Only what Ed and C.J. have said. But I'll keep my eyes peeled and my ears open as always."

"Thanks, Gil." Poppy waved as she pulled away.

35: ROAD TRIP

Poppy pulled into Mary Ellen's driveway at about nine o'clock the next morning. The plan was to stop at Starbucks before heading south on I-75 and arrive at the convent just after lunch. Poppy tooted the horn, and Mary Ellen walked out of her garage with a suitcase, a tote bag, a lunch box, a purse, and a large piece of cardboard.

Poppy couldn't believe her eyes. This was a one-night, if that, quick trip to Ohio. Poppy slid open the back doors. Now it was Mary Ellen who couldn't believe her eyes. The seats were covered with leashes, dog treats in various plastic bags (hopefully those were dog treats), a dog bowl, gallon bottles of water, fur, and mud. The floor was equally covered with Starbucks cups, used Pup Cups (Babycakes's treat of choice), food wrappers, and dirty towels. The friends looked at each other over the seat.

"Um, I'll just slide my suitcase between the seats and lay this," she said, pointing to the cardboard, "on the seat. Can I move some of the dog stuff?" She was trying not to sound judgy, but wow, this was a mess.

"Well, sure, I guess," said Poppy. "I didn't expect you to bring so much. What is all that?"

"My suitcase, obviously. The tote is for my shoes for tomorrow and a few books. Oh, and my hair straightener, which was still a little warm. The lunch bag has snacks. This is a road trip. My purse and the board," Mary Ellen cheerfully concluded.

"The board?"

"I'll explain later. Where is your stuff?" Mary Ellen looked around for what Poppy packed.

"Isn't there a backpack right there? And my purse is up front. Did you say you have shoes in the tote? Aren't you wearing shoes?" Poppy knew this was a silly question as soon as it left her mouth.

"Well, the shoes in the tote match the outfit I'll wear tomorrow." With that straightened out, Mary Ellen opened the passenger door. The seat was hairy and crummy but instead of making a big deal out of the car situation, she got in, closed the door, and buckled her seat belt.

Poppy reversed out of the driveway, and they were off. They did the Starbucks run as planned and hopped on I-75. At this time of day, traffic was sparse, so Poppy set the cruise at seventy and turned on an audiobook. Both women were fond of Richard Osman and hadn't read his latest book, *The Bullet that Missed*.

At the first rest stop in Ohio, they stopped to use the restroom and get another Starbucks. Mary Ellen had brought muffins for a snack, so they sat there enjoying the muffins and tanking up on a second caffeinated double espresso drink.

Poppy wiped the crumbs off her lap onto the floor and looked over at her friend. Mary Ellen had spread out a napkin on her lap, so her cleanup was pretty easy, although she had to admit Poppy's was apparently easier. She grabbed her trash and a few pieces that were at her feet and emptied them into a trash can on the sidewalk.

When Mary Ellen got back in the car, Poppy had the piece of cardboard spread open. It was a large trifold presentation-style cardboard. Poppy looked at Mary Ellen quizzically. "What is this?"

"It's our clue board. I know C.J. is a fine officer and an important member of our community, but the look on her face when I rolled out the mah-jongg rug wasn't one of admiration. I thought this looked more professional. It also has more space. We not only are looking at two murders, but we need space for the missing-heir hunt. What do you think?"

Mary Ellen truly admired Poppy's opinion. She was very smart and logical despite the disaster of a car.

Poppy gave it a good once-over and pronounced, "Mary Ellen, this is perfect. It's an easy way to assemble information and make connections. Thanks for thinking of it."

She pulled out of the rest stop and noted, "Next stop? The Sisters of Mercy Convent."

36: CONVENT GIRLS

Poppy and Mary Ellen arrived at a rundown building that looked like it had been built in the 1940s—not old enough to be some kind of interesting architecture, not new enough to look great, but just the right age to accurately say, "I'm down on my luck. Try not to put your foot through the porch when you ring the front door."

They eyeballed it from the weed-infested parking lot, temporarily taking Mary Ellen's mind off the smell of old meatball sandwiches Poppy had taken from the Subway dumpster to entice Munchie, Chuckie, and Roscoe. As well, Mary Ellen was acutely aware that when she stood up, there was going to be no way she could avoid a conspicuous wiping of crumbs off her rear end. But she was beyond the point of worrying about offending her best friend. Why did her car always smell like an unrefrigerated deli? How could she live like that? When Mary Ellen opened the passenger door and stepped out, she heard the crunch of cellophane from Nonni's biscotti wrappers that had somehow stuck to her shoe. "Really," she thought, "this is nuts."

Poppy hopped out of the driver's door with nothing stuck to her ass and not having to pick debris off her shoes. She not so subtly eyed Mary Ellen and thought, Geez, she's normally so put together. What the heck. She watched her friend struggle to stand on one foot and use a wadded-up Kleenex to wipe off the bottom of her shoe, which somehow looked as though it had a piece of meat on it. Poppy was concerned that her friend was slipping a little, but they had business to do. She thought it was a really good thing she had driven as they walked toward the rickety porch, after eyeballing a 1960s-era Chrysler, also down on its luck.

The front door was huge and heavy, with a small window where the view could be opened or closed from the inside. To the left of the door was an old-fashioned pull, presumably to ring a bell inside the building. And affixed to the front door was a huge cross and a plaque saying, "Welcome to the Home of the Sisters of Mercy." Both thought at least they were in the right place.

A relatively young nun, probably around the age of forty-five, opened the door and seemed surprised to see the two visitors. She had on a pair of jeans, a tee shirt, and a traditional nun's veil. She looked curiously at the two women on her porch.

Mary Ellen introduced the two of them and asked if they could possibly speak to the head of the Sisters of Mercy. The nun introduced herself as Sister Bernadette and explained that she had been working in the back garden most of the day, where they grew vegetables. She indicated they should come in and explained that Mother Genevieve was there and might see them if they'd please wait by the door a short time.

Poppy noted to Mary Ellen, "There's no one else around!" Indeed, the place was crazy quiet and felt almost unoccupied.

"Perhaps some of them go to work these days," said Mary Ellen.

Sister Bernadette reappeared and ushered them into a dusty office that did house an early-generation Mac computer on the desk. Mother Genevieve looked to be in her early eighties.

The elderly nun filled them in on the fact that the two of them living there were the end of the line of the Sisters of Mercy. Their calling of taking in out-of-wedlock girls who were pregnant and placing the babies in good homes had fallen by the wayside over the years to more structured institutions overseen by local authorities—like the Child and Family Welfare Agency. Not to mention the easier access to birth control and lack of shame raising a child out of wedlock. All this made their mission antiquated. She confirmed she had indeed been there since she was sixteen and rose in the ranks to being in full administrative charge of the operations for the last half-century. There was a time, she explained, when they were pretty busy and needed, and indeed were called to help and serve.

Poppy and Mary Ellen exchanged turns telling all about Virginia Stanley having been one of their "girls" around fifty years ago, and that she gave birth there to a child and they knew nothing more than that. But this fortunate child just might inherit millions if they could locate him or her. However, Virginia herself had been murdered in the tourist town three hours north of where the Sisters of Mercy lived.

While Poppy and Mary Ellen had expected a wall of

bureaucratic resistance to releasing confidential information, this wasn't a bureaucracy. This was just Mother Genevieve. And she was saddened to hear that one of their one-time girls named Virginia had been brutally killed. Even after all these years, that hurt.

Father Bob was right on the mark. These nuns would be offended by this brutality and therefore might be motivated to cooperate.

She explained that all paper records had been painstakingly converted to the personal computer they saw before them to preserve the records. It had taken years for the two nuns to key in all the information.

It took a while—this was no Google search—but Mother Genevieve came up with the record showing that Virginia had given birth to a healthy boy fifty-five years ago who was immediately placed with a farm family in southern Michigan. Virginia never knew whether she had a boy or a girl or where the child was placed because that was just how they did things back then. The baby was whisked away, and the adopted parents were given an absolute guarantee of privacy and protection—and the nuns weren't further involved.

She was able to print the information that she had. The mechanical ghost in the office set up a racket with what could be the last working dot matrix printer in the Midwest, banging away each dot like a tiny hammer blow to the brain. They also had the names of the farmers who adopted the infant.

After having a cup of tea and a conversation about how things had changed quite a bit—whether one thought that was good or not—Mary Ellen and Poppy headed toward the Honda and back to Michigan to talk to Chief Ed. Poppy had convinced Mary Ellen that they had plenty of time to drive back that night and talk to Barney, despite all of Mary Ellen's careful and thorough packing. They never set eyes on Sister Bernadette again. Presumably Sister Bernadette was in her jeans and veil, trying to make something grow in the old tired dirt, or perhaps she'd run errands in that piece of Detroit iron that had been moved from the parking lot, a Chrysler "as big as a whale," as the B-52s once sang.

•••

Mother Genevieve stood at the window, watching the two women visitors—themselves making for an extraordinary day—depart, noting the dog stickers on the back of Poppy's van with a small shake of her head. And she stood there quite a bit longer, lost in thought, lost in years. The complications of the work of the Sisters of Mercy weren't a new concept to her. Every child that came through the door leaving without her child was both a success and a tragedy that never escaped her.

The choices for a pregnant fifteen-year-old were grim. She had absolutely no guilt and some sinful pride, she supposed, about the work there. While the choices had changed during the intervening years, giving girls and women more control, a pregnant fifteen-year-old was still a child full of challenges ahead.

She thought of the one who returned, who became for all intents and purposes her daughter, Sister Bernadette, who had been a blessing in her life. While Poppy and Mary Ellen seemed free as soaring eagles to the old nun, there were those who preferred the lives of house sparrows.

•••

Sister Bernadette remembered her experience there during that tender fifteenth year as literally lifesaving, and returned when she could to join the women. And never left. Meanwhile, she had indeed taken the old Chrysler to the store as Mary Ellen and Poppy had guessed, after listening in on enough of the conversation the visitors were having. Would she approve of her own son's life being disrupted, perhaps causing him to discover maybe for the first time that his parents weren't biologically related, if he could inherit a large sum of money?

She put the two bags of groceries in the enormous back seat and climbed behind the wheel. "Maybe," she said to herself, as she stomped on the accelerator, heading back to Mother Genevieve, "and maybe not."

37: THE ALTMUEHL RIVER ROOM

Mary and Mike, arguably one of the happiest married couples anyone knew, had agreed to go check out the space at the Lodge for the mah-jongg tournament. Mary Ellen had an appointment with Poppy's attorney, according to the message on their phone.

Mary said, "Hope all is well with Poppy."

Mike said, "She's probably updating some legal stuff, something we ought to think about as well."

"Ummm, or maybe Poppy's attorney is a new boyfriend. I thought I heard that she has a houseguest."

Mike shrugged. "Let's not jump to conclusions. We'll check out the room and have breakfast at Oma's."

"Great idea."

The Bavarian Inn Lodge was easiest reached by the Holz-Brücke Bridge over the Cass River. The bridge built in 1980 by the Zehnder families was the largest covered bridge in Michigan. It allowed both cars and pedestrians a spectacular way to approach the Lodge, by far the largest hotel and conference center in town. Mary and Mike parked in front of that wing.

On this day, the lobby was quite crowded with a line of people. Looking around the line, Mary spotted Dorothy Zehnder, the matriarch of the Bavarian Inn, sitting at a table by the bay windows. She had just celebrated her one hundredth birthday. She still appeared in the kitchen regularly, supervising the staff, especially with some of her signature dishes.

Mary nudged Mike. "That's Dorothy and she's signing her cookbook. Let's get copies for all the girls in the family for Christmas."

Mike agreed. "Great idea. Let's see what's up."

They opened the door to the Altmuehl River Room. It was set up for their tournament with six square tables that would seat four each. On the far wall was a long table that would hold the buffet lunch. The room was perfect.

Mike and Mary closed the door and got in line for cookbooks. After getting ten books personalized (Mary came from a large family), they carried them out to the car. They then walked back so Mike could have some delicious potato pancakes. They were immediately waylaid by some guy selling items in one of the smaller available rooms.

"Welcome, I'm Adam Brown, cheese connoisseur and kitchen implement purveyor. After writing for *Cheese and Wine Magazine* and working with some of the finest chefs, I have developed my own line of kitchen knives and gadgets that make all kitchens a better place. Let me show you around. Over here I have my line of cheese specific knives and …"

Mike interrupted Adam. "Looks amazing. We're on our way to lunch, but thanks." As he and Mary turned to leave, they almost bumped into a blonde lady with a big smile.

"She sure seems happy to see Mr. Brown and his knives. Let's go eat."

After a delicious lunch, they strolled back to the lobby. It appeared that Dorothy was finished signing cookbooks for the day. Mr. Brown was standing at the table, talking to her. "I think it would be great if we collaborated. I could use my utensils to make some of your recipes. A match made in Little Bavaria. What do you think?"

Dorothy's daughter Judy was packing up books off to the side. She straightened up. "Mom really doesn't need to collaborate, Mr. Brown. Thanks for your offer."

Adam didn't really take this information well. "But new equipment will make old recipes more interesting to young cooks. I know it will be a hit. And with my credentials...." But even Adam Brown recognized the resolute look on both Judy's and Dorothy's faces. He turned around and headed back to the Danube River Room.

Mike and Mary realized they had been blatantly eavesdropping and turned around and left.

Mary said, "That's guy's a little smarmy, don't you think?"

Mike nodded.

38: THE GIRLS REPORT TO BARNEY

The conversation between Mary Ellen and Poppy on the way back didn't include comments about excess baggage or unseemly amounts of trash.

"Imagine what that place was like back when Virginia was 'in confinement,' as they used to say there," Poppy said.

Mary Ellen was imagining. "I bet the place was packed with girls 'in trouble,' as they called it. Families at home lying about where their daughter was, while everyone knew it and no one said it out loud, and everyone's son went on with his life."

Poppy chimed in, "I remember a kid down the street that I knew had a cousin come stay with her. I guess her parents weren't the convent sort, but they sent their daughter out of state. My parents, I think I was around thirteen or fourteen at the time, explained what was going on. They explained why it was best for everyone all around. Her name was Meredith and she had visited before and was a nice kid. I liked her. The adultness of what she was going through shook me."

"Did she just go home like nothing happened after the baby was born?"

"Yes. And even though she and her cousin Jeannie and I spent time together, no one spoke of what was going on. Two years later, my parents sat me down on a warm summer day on the patio and said they had some news about Meredith."

"Oh boy," said Mary Ellen.

"I said to them, 'She's dead, isn't she?' My parents were shocked. But she was dead. She drowned accidentally on a family swimming outing. Anyway, that was the story and I chose to believe it, hard as even that was."

"But you don't believe it."

"No. I guess I don't. I wonder if the nuns were able to do a better job than Meredith's family managed. We don't know, for instance, if the girls had outside visitors or what."

Mary Ellen pointed out, "It's clear that Mother Genevieve cared about those girls."

"Yeah. That much is clear."

●●●

They arrived back in town by eight o'clock that evening after stopping for a burger on the way. Lights were on in Poppy's house as they usually were during the short amount of time that Barney was staying there. Barney worked. A lot.

They had decided that they'd have a short meeting with Barney before Mary Ellen went home to Todd while the visit with what was left of the Sisters of Mercy was fresh in their minds. The vision that greeted them was Barney lying on the couch reading a pile of papers of whatever sort, with Babycakes snuggled on his stomach. She clearly was in a quandary whether to jump off and greet Poppy like she normally would, or risk leaving Barney to his own devices. She had sort of adopted him, that was clear. She opted for standing up and wagging her little corkscrew tail at Poppy and Mary Ellen. That elicited an "ouch!" from Barney, who set the papers aside.

"Well," Barney said, cutting the small talk down to zero, "was the trip worthwhile? Did Father Bob send you to the right place?"

Poppy looked at the KFC box on the coffee table. She thought maybe Babycakes had a little grease on her nose. "Barney? How on Earth is it that you're in Frankenmuth, where the best chicken in the state is served in multiple locations, and I see a KFC box? You'd have to make an actual effort to find a box of KFC around here." And why is it, thought Poppy, that the notion of KFC kept popping up these days? So peculiar. She glanced at her dog, who was licking her own nose.

Mary Ellen took the lead and explained the entire visit to Barney. His concentration was one hundred percent. She told him about everything, from the disrepair of the facilities to the dot matrix printer banging out the information he was hoping they'd find.

"So. What you're telling me," said Barney formulating his thought precisely, "is you found out where and when Virginia Stanley's child, a boy as it turns out, was born. And furthermore, you have there—" he emphasized by tapping the printout they laid on the table, "you have the names of the adoptive parents as well as their address at the time of the adoption. Is that right?"

Mary Ellen and Poppy both affirmed simultaneously the accuracy of that. Poppy added, "We need to go see Chief Ed, Barney. This isn't just a hunt for an heir. This is all part and parcel—or at least could be—to two murder cases here in town."

"That's exactly right," agreed Barney. "This is definitely information the police need to know, right down to what's in the will, everything we've got here."

•••

So that was exactly what the three of them did the next morning, meeting with both the chief and C.J. Chief Ed took all this in, sorting out possibilities as the story went along. He concluded this: 1) Virginia was likely killed by a niece, nephew, or in-law who thought they'd inherit; or 2) just as likely perhaps, there was her designated heir running around who had a less than pleasant life and he killed her; or 3) none of this was relevant to her death, and Clare likely killed her simply out of opportunity and revenge. And where exactly did that get them with the murder of the carriage driver?

Ed told them C.J. would track down the couple who adopted Virginia's son, if possible. And Ed invited himself to the meeting where Barney explained exactly what and who the will provided for to her relatives over at the Residenz.

Meantime, Poppy and Mary Ellen decided they just needed some coffee.

39: THE MAH-JONGG TOURNAMENT

Todd drove Mary Ellen up to the Lodge the next morning.
This way he could help carry in all the tiles, rugs, prizes, and
table goodies. Todd was not a player, but he frequently did
mah-jongg errands. Yesterday, he had gone to Saginaw to
buy individual bamboo shoots for each of the participants.
Mary Ellen wrapped them in red tissue paper and planned
on placing four at every table.

They had stopped at the Kaffee Haus on their way so that
Mary Ellen had her large cappuccino. Once the car had been
emptied, Todd said he was going to look for coffee. "Plain
black coffee in Styrofoam without my name written on the
cup." Mary Ellen hung up a red-and-gold dragon banner
giving the room a festive vibe.

Mary and Mike arrived just then. Mary Ellen greeted them.
"Welcome, and thanks for coming early. Todd went in search
of coffee. We just need to pass out schedules and groupings.
Why don't we set up our tables with racks and tiles? That way
we can help others who might be running a little late."

Mike grabbed the papers with the schedules and groupings
and put four on each table. Mary followed with a mason jar

containing the bamboo shoots. Mary Ellen started arranging the prize table.

Mary came over to help. "Wow! Those prizes are amazing. A mah-jongg set is first prize?"

Mary Ellen said, "That was heavily discounted by Linda Li. Several of us bought her limited-edition sets and when I told her of our tournament, she extended an excellent discount code for us. There are mah-jongg rugs, cheese knives …"

"Speaking of cheese knives," Todd said as he walked in, holding a plain white Styrofoam cup of presumably hot black coffee, "the guy next door has quite a store set up. He sells knives and is going to be cooking with Dorothy Zehnder to show his tools of the trade."

Mike and Mary exchanged looks. "I'm pretty sure he isn't cooking with Dorothy. He was here yesterday pitching his idea. Dorothy and Judy were having none of it. He seems a little full of himself," Mike said.

"Well, I bought a little gadget for your prize table," Todd said, holding out a bright-yellow plastic contraption.

"That is so nice! Thanks, honey. What is it?" Mary Ellen put it with the other prizes. You can't have too many prizes at a mah-jongg tournament, they were all thinking.

Todd grinned sheepishly. "No idea. It looked cool and I assume if anyone cooks, they'll know."

Mary Ellen held it up for Mike to see. "Any ideas?"

Mike shook his head. "Looks interesting, though."

The players started to arrive. Everyone knew everyone, since this wasn't an open tournament but one for the groups who played in town. Excitement was in the air. By three o'clock they'd had a delicious lunch, played a day's worth of games, tallied points, and the lucky ones collected prizes.

Mary Ellen was thrilled. Everyone congratulated beaming winners while the non-winners kidded about the missing jokers.

Mary Ellen packed up her tiles and started to text Todd that she needed a ride home. Instead, she got a text from Poppy. "Time for us to meet Ed and Barney at the Residenz for the reading of the will. You're about done, right? I'll pick you up at the front door in five minutes."

"Great," Mary Ellen muttered. "Another chance to ride in Poppy's car." She grimaced a little. She wheeled her cart from the room and practically collided with Col. Sanders. "Oh, I'm sorry. I wasn't looking where I was going," she said.

"No problem. How was your tournament? Was the olive pitter a hit? Your husband said you were playing for prizes."

"Oh, it was a great hit." Mary Ellen needed to remember to tell Joan that she had won an olive pitter before she gave it to Goodwill. "Excuse me. My ride is here."

•••

Mary Ellen rushed out the door, dragging her cart. The van door slid open and Poppy called out, "Hop in."

Mary Ellen carefully put her cart into the back, trying to ignore the leashes, treats, poop bags, and who knew what else. She hopped into the passenger side.

"Just talked to Col. Sanders. He's selling kitchen stuff in the Danube River Room."

"Well, that answers that. He's just a salesman pushing his goods. This will reading should be interesting. Chief Ed and C.J. are going to be there, too. Barney drove separately, not sure why." Mary Ellen gave a slight eye roll out the passenger window.

In no time, they had reached the Residenz. Barney's car and Chief Ed's cruiser were already in the driveway, so the friends hurried in.

40: THE READING OF THE WILL

Some people in the crowded room knew what was in the will—Chief Ed, C.J., Barney, Mary Ellen, and Poppy. They almost outnumbered the family consisting of Joe and his wife, Amelia, Ned and his fiancée, Arrabella, Nelly, and Nora. The family had been "fussing and feuding" as the old saying goes even before Virginia Stanley was slaughtered on her scenic carriage ride around town. But the one thing they could come together on was they didn't want the "big reveal" of Aunt Virginia's will without liquor. That added one more person to the room, Jim the bartender, who worked for the Bavarian Lodge conglomerate.

Chief Ed, on the edge after not one but two fast killings in his town, had squad cars on deck parked conspicuously outside the Residenz in case the contents of the will pushed a killer over an emotional cliff.

As if that weren't enough people, Barney had also reserved a person from the Lodge to operate AV equipment since Virginia wanted the last word one more time. Barney could have done without that, but they didn't call it a will for nothing—it was Virginia's will as to how this would be handled. Indeed, Barney was going to make his way up to Frankenmuth anyway, just not this soon. And truth be told, he wasn't opposed entirely to a little razzle-dazzle with his presentations. It was just going to be very odd that the person asking for the reading intended to be there alive AND still be on video. Virginia was one strange old bird in her own right, Barney thought, but she had been his strange bird, and he felt obligated to see this through.

Barney sighed to himself and took to the floor. "I'm Barney Mead, your aunt's attorney from Liberty, Ohio, and I'm very sorry for your loss. I've spoken to Joe on the phone to arrange this presentation of Virginia's will."

"Hey, wait!" It was Ned, suddenly standing. "What are they doing here?" he asked as he nodded in the direction of Mary Ellen and Poppy. "I thought they worked in the kitchen or something. Do all our family legal matters have to be public fodder? What's next? Why not just publish the will in the *Frankenmuth News*. Hell, why not *The New York Times*?"

The family muttered because Ned asked an uncharacteristically good question. Nora and Nelly called from their spot next to the bar, where Jim was refreshing their drinks, "Yeah! Good point, Ned!"

Barney cut them off. "They are on my payroll as investigators, which is what they do. I have no idea why they were in the kitchen previously, but they are here now in case they need to answer something we hadn't anticipated." Chief Ed nodded agreement, and even C.J.—not Poppy and Mary Ellen's biggest fan—was happy to see Barney Mead control the conversation.

"OK," Barney continued. "Your aunt planned to have me show this video of her telling you her wishes about the distribution of her property in the event of her death," Barney said, spieling off the lawyer language regarding wills automatically. "She felt too frail to do it in person herself, so she arranged a nice vacation so that you would know what is in the will."

Joe spoke up. "That's freaking weird, Barney!" he exploded, using Barney's first name freely because he had forgotten "Mead" already.

Barney responded, "Let's not get stuck characterizing your aunt's presentation choices. I'll admit it's unusual what she requested here. But I assure you what she didn't want to happen was to get murdered in a wagon on Main Street."

Chief Ed, Mary Ellen, C.J., Poppy, and even the bartender all simultaneously flinched at the word "wagon." Jim downed a quick one off his own bar cart.

Barney said, "Can I continue now, please?" Barney glanced sideways toward the bartender but couldn't think of a professional way to ask for a snort of his own.

The family simmered down for the moment.

A twin stood up, three-olive martini in hand. "Wait! Why is there all this police presence? The chief of police? His right-hand investigator, apparently?" (skeptical glance at C.J. included). "And squad cars within sight out the window? You cannot possibly think that anyone in the family—all of whom were right here during Virginia's murder—did it? We have total alibis. And you've got the kitchen girl locked up for drugging our aunt, right? Why isn't she arrested for murder? I don't get you people! It's bad enough we have to watch a videotape of Virginia after she's been killed, but we have to share that experience with law enforcement. Why on Earth?"

"Who cares," yelled Joe, "whichever one you are! In a world of mysteries, why do you and your sister still dress the same, as though you were three years old? I'm just enraged that we need to listen to a videotape of our aunt at all to find out 'the final disposition of her assets,' as this guy keeps saying—I don't care who overhears it. And when did you get so picky? You and that Col. Sanders cheesy guy haven't been all that subtle or private, as I can attest since our rooms share a wall."

Nelly—as it happened—sucked in her breath. Before she could respond to this tongue lashing, Chief Ed said, "Let's bring the temperature down a notch, please. And remember that the police are working two active murder cases at the moment and one of those is your aunt. And the other is her carriage driver. Can we please just let her attorney proceed?"

Barney grabbed the opportunity to continue as though nothing peculiar were happening. "OK. Let's just focus, please. Everyone. Miss Marshall," he said, nodding to the AV person, "can you play Virginia's video, please? I would appreciate it if everyone can save their remarks until this is over so that I can answer any questions—and really there shouldn't be very many questions—at the end of this required presentation."

Nora stage whispered, "Since the person requiring this farce is dead, who exactly is requiring it—Mr. Barney?"

A split second later, Virginia's voice boomed from the sound system, immediately the focus of everyone's attention in the room, other than C.J.'s. She was taking notes on what the family was doing.

All other eyes were on Virginia, dressed in smart slacks and a red jacket and comfortably seated in her own living room. Although she wasn't seen drinking on the video, they couldn't help but notice a highball glass with fresh ice on the end table beside her.

"Hello, my dear nieces and nephews. I wanted you to be fully aware of my intentions regarding the disposition of my property in the event of my death."

"Sweet mother of God," said Joe, with a hostile glance at Barney, who apparently didn't mind or even notice Joe's anger.

Virginia's voice continued. "There are things about my past that none of you know. And since none of my nieces and nephews ever bothered to get close to me, I have had no confidants within the family. In all honesty, you're a self-centered little bunch, although I wish you well. But I think when you hear the facts, you'll at least understand."

Both Ed and Barney were thinking that this woman looked like she could go another twenty years and have time to yank around the family numerous times before her last estate plan was put into effect.

"When I was fifteen—and picture that this was some time ago—I fell in love with an eighteen-year-old boy at my high school. While I pictured a life of endless love together forever, he was simply interested in casual sex he could brag to his friends about. I was very young and naïve."

Ned said in an exasperated voice, "Where on Earth is this going?"

Joe said, "Shut up so we can all find out, Ned."

Virginia added, "I am sure you all see where this is going." Ned muttered under his breath, finally whipped into submission by his aunt's voice.

"And you're right," continued Virginia. "I found myself pregnant and he acted as though he never knew my name. So, and I will spare you the fine details, my parents sent me away to stay with some nuns until I had the child whom they gave away."

Murmuring overtook the room. Now they really could see where this was going, and no one liked it a bit.

"Well, I certainly hope you've had a great time in Frankenmuth," said Virginia, "because this will be the last vacation on me."

"You bitch," hollered both twins at once.

Ned's fiancée followed that comment with, "I told you all this would happen!"

"I never knew whether my child was a boy or girl. It was a child I didn't want by a boy I came to despise. And this child was adopted out. It is my final wish—"

"More final than you know!" hollered Joe, who had the attention of Chief Ed by this time.

"—that my assets be spent—as much as necessary—in locating this adult child of mine and that he or she will then inherit the balance of my estate, and it is my express wish that no one else shall benefit from my estate.

"My attorney, Mr. Mead, will explain to you that, contrary to what the family thinks, I do have issue to inherit. And that means a direct blood line. While this child lost the right to inheritance by being adopted, I can restore it by writing him or her into the will, and my blood issue becomes my heir. Please find your own ways home. In the event that this child is deceased or cannot be located up to a year and one day following my death, the remainder of my assets shall go to whichever niece or nephew draws the high card in a normal deck of fifty-two at the office of my attorney, who will oversee the event, because I'm here to tell you, life is a crapshoot and aces are high."

Everyone sucked air at once. Ned picked up the chair he was sitting in and flung it through the glass patio doors. Joe punched Ned in the nose for probably a thousand reasons, none very specific to this situation. Blood was all over, and Ned's nose clearly broken. And Ned's fiancée threw her drink at one of the twins (she despised them both, so it didn't matter which one) who ducked, leaving C.J. on the receiving end of a drink in the face.

All of this took very few seconds and not much more time than that for the squad cars to empty out, and officers, who started moving when the glass doors broke, to begin cuffing people and putting them in the backs of cruisers. "Everyone goes to the station," said Chief Ed, "and we'll figure the list of charges when we get them all there." One of the officers pointed to Poppy and Mary Ellen, his eyebrows raised in a question mark. "No, not them, and leave the bartender," said Ed. The AV lady had exited the room the second the video ended. Barney just looked, apparently, like someone you wouldn't arrest.

Barney turned to Mary Ellen and Poppy and winked. "That went great. Let's go out to dinner tonight. We have an heir to find."

41: POLICE STATION, PART DEUX

Ed led the parade of squad cars to the station. He had Joe in the back seat and Ned was handcuffed in the front, holding a bloody bar towel to his nose. Ed knew his car would be out of commission tomorrow to be thoroughly cleaned.

On arrival, Ed put everyone in the conference room with a stern warning that if they could not behave, they were all going to the county lockup. He suggested that everyone sit in silence. His voice made it clear there was no choice.

"Buddy and Tom, you stand guard in the conference room," Ed said to his two officers. "C.J., let's go in and see if we can take the temperature of the room. If they are calm enough, I'd like to release them back to the Residenz. As a backup, can you call Judy and see if there are a few extra rooms at the Lodge? That way, if we have to separate people, we have an option. She can add them to the Stanley bill."

Ed and C.J. went to their respective offices. Ed flipped the switch so he could hear what was going on. Several years ago, a suspect wrongly accused a police officer of threatening him during interrogation. Ed had a speaker and remote feed installed for the protection of everyone who used that room.

It seemed that Ed's "suggestion" had worked. Other than heavy sighs and restless sounds, all was quiet. Ed picked up the Stanley file and left his office just as C.J. was coming down the hallway.

"Judy already knew about the door and has workmen up at the Residenz. Also, there are three rooms available in case they are needed. They are in your name. Shall we see what they have to say?"

Everyone was sitting quietly. Buddy had brought Ned some ice and a clean towel. Tom had taken all the handcuffs off so they could sit comfortably. They looked a little sheepish. As Ed knew from the police chief in Liberty, none of these people were public nuisances.

"So, let me begin." Ed stood at the head of the table. "You will pay for the damage done to the Residenz. If I decide that you all can't stay in one place civilly, you will pay for additional rooms. Ned, do you want to press charges?"

Ned shook his head. Arrabella grabbed his hand and gave it a squeeze. It appeared that they had calmed down. Ed and C.J. were relieved that they weren't transporting the group to Saginaw.

Joe cleared his throat. "Chief, I apologize. We are a little hot headed, but we aren't bad people. This will reading was eerie. Seeing and hearing my dead aunt, like she had planned to be there, put us all on edge. Then hearing that all her money was going to a long-lost child. Honestly. I was really counting on inheriting something. I would have been able to go to the bank and use my future windfall as collateral for my new business venture."

Ned spoke through the towel. "I, too, wanted money for a play I was going to produce starring Arrabella. We both were hoping that Aunt Gin would help us out."

Nelly nodded. "We thought Aunt Gin would be proud of us owning a successful business. We would have liked to think that she wanted to reward our hard work."

Chief Ed nodded. "It was quite a theatrical presentation. If you think you can all spend the night without fighting, I am inclined to take you back to the Residenz." As he spoke, he flipped open the Stanley file. He had a form that he had quickly filled out detailing who was there and the result. He noticed the DNA results that were on top. He had never really looked at them. He had relied on the summary that the officer had given him.

Everyone stood up, and C.J. said that they could probably squeeze into two patrol cars. Buddy took Joe, Amelia, and Nelly. C.J. took Ned, Arrabella, and Nora. As they left, Ed sat down. He had a puzzled look on his face. Only the males' tests had been expedited. None of the DNA matched the material under Mark's fingernail. But there were three tests. There were only two nephews. The test results indicated that all males had familial traits. Ed slapped the table. The third test was Jim the bartender.

42: LORELEI LOUNGE

The released family opened the door to the Residenz. They were a subdued group and looked tired and, in the case of Ned, battered.

Joe commented, "Looks like the staff has been in to clean up our mess and board up the broken door."

They all headed into the kitchen as no one had eaten anything since lunch. The refrigerator still had some leftovers from their meals. Amelia and Arrabella started putting things out on the counter. Ned grabbed some ice and wrapped it in a towel to put on his nose. Nelly went back into the Great Room and immediately returned.

"Well, looks like the bar is closed. Whoever tidied up took all the alcohol with them. We have been cut off." She looked at her twin and said, "Nora, let's go over to the Lorelei Lounge for a quiet drink. No offense, I think we need some space, and I would like a cocktail."

They walked out the back door and across the lawn to the Lodge. The Lorelei Lounge was quiet, and the girls sat at a table away from the bar. A server quickly asked if they'd like menus. "Actually, I'd like a gin and tonic with lime," said Nelly, looking at Nora, "in honor of Aunt Gin."

"And I'll have a Bombay Sapphire martini with three blue-cheese-stuffed olives," Nora chimed in. "And a pretzel. You do offer those lovely warm pretzels?"

"We do, and I'll have those drinks right up. Thanks, ladies."

Nora and Nelly sat quietly until their drinks and pretzel arrived. "To Aunt Gin!" They raised their glasses and toasted their aunt. "Without whom we would not have had such an incredible vacation."

Nora said, "I usually post about my travels on Facebook, but I think two murders and two trips to the police station may not show up."

Nelly took another sip of her drink. "Well, I am sorry Ned and Joe were so disappointed. I didn't realize how much they were counting on Virginia's money. I think when we get home, we should invite them to the office for a financial review, see if we can help them out."

"Great idea, Nelly. Nelly? What are you looking at?" Nora turned around to see Adam Brown headed their way. Nelly was waving him over.

"What a beautiful sight to behold. Good evening, ladies. May I join you?"

Nelly turned to her sister. "Nora, I'd like to introduce you to Adam Brown. He's an entrepreneur from Ohio. Adam, how are your business dealings in town going?"

Nora shook Adam's hand and said to Nelly, "Actually, Adam and I know each other. He had business in Liberty and our paths crossed several times."

Nelly looked at Nora. "Oh, he has dealings here as well." The girls exchanged glances, noting that Adam was shifting uncomfortably in his seat. He clearly did not have the upper hand.

"Are you celebrating something?" he asked, changing the subject. "Hey, I have some of my famous cheese blend here in my pocket." He opened his coat that did indeed have lots of pockets and pulled out a can of something. "This will be amazing on that pretzel. Give it a try." He squirted some on the pretzel in the middle of the table.

"Oh, my, that's got quite an aftertaste," said Nora, taking another healthy swallow of her martini.

"Actually, we aren't celebrating. As you know, our Aunt Virginia was killed, brutally murdered, and her attorney came to read the will this afternoon. Unexpectedly, our brother, cousin, and ourselves were not the heirs," Nelly paused.

Adam cleared his throat. "Really? I thought you were her only relatives. She didn't leave her money to a cat or something silly like that?"

"No, but she did leave all her money to a child she had in her teens. None of us knew anything about it. I guess her attorney has some information and will be looking for the ..."

Adam was choking. He had turned red and was motioning for a glass of water. Nora gave him her martini, which he downed in one swallow.

"Whew, choked on that pretzel. I should go upstairs, ladies. I'm sorry I ruined your evening." With that, Adam was gone.

"That seemed abrupt. I'm going to order another cocktail since mine was used for first aid." Nora motioned to the server. Nelly picked up the can of cheese and the girls started to laugh, both glad they came to the lounge tonight.

43: DOWN ON THE FARM

Frankenmuth, for all its tourist town Little Bavaria delights, was also a farming community. You could not drive into Frankenmuth from any direction without driving past farms. Everything from wheat to the big-industry sugar beets to big-industry corn to a substantial money crop of beans grew in all directions from the town. It was interesting to watch the yearly progression of farming on the thousands of acres spread out over the bucolic flatland of the Saginaw Valley.

Still within the city limits and mere blocks north of the Visitor Center in town towered the silos of Star of the West. Farmers drove their trucks full of grain straight from farms to be stored and then distributed by Star of the West. The bright-yellow trucks delivered the grain far beyond Frankenmuth.

Barney, Poppy, and Mary Ellen had the names of the farm couple who adopted the son of Virginia Stanley, now in his mid-fifties if he was still around. Although the information was passed on to the police, that didn't stop Barney and his investigators from continuing their search. One thing Barney knew was that it was rare that police raced over to talk to lawyers when they discovered something.

What they were able to find out through public records was that Bill and Dolores Schmidt, who were likely the same William and Dolores Schmidt who adopted the Stanley infant, had a decent-sized farm east of Frankenmuth, a few miles over, by the rural community of Millington.

Poppy was working the computers and found the obituary of William Schmidt from a few years ago, indicating that his wife Dolores had survived him, along with their only child, James Schmidt. Poppy believed that James Schmidt was their missing heir, and Barney and Mary Ellen agreed that this was likely. What they didn't realize was that the police were circling toward the same conclusion at nearly the same time through different means, namely DNA results taken from everyone at the Residenz when Virginia was murdered. Considering that the Stanley family members were thought of as tourists getting together to share a vacation and perhaps a surprise from Ohio, it was peculiar, as Barney, Mary Ellen, Poppy, C.J, and Ed were all half an inch from discovering that all roads were leading to a nondescript Millington farm.

Poppy said to Barney, who was once again spending some serious time sharing an unappetizing dinner with Babycakes, "What I haven't yet determined is whether Dolores is still on the farm and farming, or whether she remains in the farmhouse but leases land for other farmers to use, or even if she still owns the farm but lives somewhere else now."

Mary Ellen had checked the register of deeds office for Tuscola County and saw Dolores Schmidt's name on the farm, and that there were no liens against the land and house. Barney said, "Once we're armed with as much information as possible, it will be time to head out to the farm and see what we can learn there, especially as far as what has become of James Schmidt. That's what we really want to know."

None of the three of them had at this time begun to put together that the very same James Schmidt had worked for the Lodge as an experienced bartender for a number of years now.

Barney remarked, "Although it's difficult to say where all this is going relative to the two murders in town—if anywhere—it ought to take us very close to an heir, which is the reason I am sleeping in your spare room all this time anyway, Poppy. Great job!"

The four of them sat there thinking about the whole thing (well, Babycakes sat there munching a bite of taco from Barney and keeping her thoughts to herself), and they all had a feeling that things were about to get even more interesting.

"Girls," said Barney. Every time she heard that, Poppy felt like she was in a sitcom. "Let's set up the family Find My Phone app thing for our phones so we each can see where all three of our phones are. Since we are—albeit accidentally—involved in a murder investigation and don't know who the killer or killers are, we ought to be able to find each other in a pinch."

Poppy and Mary Ellen literally blinked at this idea since it never had occurred to either of them to track each other. Mary Ellen and Todd hadn't even turned it on to track each other. And, Poppy was thinking, Babycakes tracked the old-fashioned way—flat nose to the ground. Here she was now—smart-tracking some taco debris.

"What the heck," Mary Ellen said. "Couldn't hurt and we can always delete that app from our phones when this is all done."

They sat down and within a couple minutes were connected.

"Tomorrow morning," Barney continued, "I'm going to drive out to the Schmidt farm and see what's going on there. Mrs. Schmidt still owns the place, and it seems likely she knows where her son is, assuming she's still living there herself. Maybe I'll take Babycakes. You know she likes a good car ride."

"OK, but don't lose my dog on some farm, Barney," Poppy warned.

"She's safe with her Uncle Barney."

Both "girls" rolled their eyes. Babycakes snuffled in Barney's lap.

44: THE BARTENDER

Jim Schmidt was winding down with a drink in his efficiency apartment—after all, no one could make a drink quite like a bartender. He was a reader and always liked a good story he could get into. His reading habits tended toward international thrillers in exotic locations. He was in the middle of a Tom Clancy novel and looked forward to the escapism after such a weird day.

He was interrupted by a firm knocking on the door and a woman's voice saying, "Police!"

"What?" he said, opening the door. He recognized the officer as the woman in plain clothes he saw at the Stanley family debacle.

"I need you to come with me, Sir," C.J. said. "The chief has requested that I give you a ride to the station for a conversation."

"Do I need a lawyer? Am I under arrest? For what? What's going on here? What do you mean, give me a ride? I have a car. How about if I meet you there?"

A uniformed officer stepped out of the shadow but said nothing.

Jim was savvy enough to know he was going to the police station and he could call a lawyer from there if he needed one. He wondered about that guy from Ohio—what's his name, Barney? Barney Mead?—who managed to get everyone's underwear in a bunch in the Stanley family. He liked that guy. He seemed like a real lawyer for sure. Like one you'd almost see on TV. He'd call Barney. But since he had no idea why he was being "detained," if that was what this was, it was hard to know. One second, he was reading Tom Clancy, and the next the cops were hauling him to the world's tiniest pokey. Some day off.

He was escorted to the back of the cruiser as both C.J. and the uniform took the front seat. Off they went to the little police station that had seen more action in the last few days than in the past ten years.

Jim wasn't searched, other than a cursory pat down for a gun, and he wasn't cuffed, and they didn't respond when he asked if he were under arrest. So he was sure he wasn't because they didn't do any of that. No Miranda rights. Just kind of an Uber ride a few blocks away. He decided he'd be like Jack Reacher in one of those books he loved to read by Lee Child and say as little as possible while he tried to figure out what was going on. He had read multiple times that the thing lawyers wished most was that their clients in custody would just shut up. He could do that.

By the time he was sitting reasonably comfortably in an interview room—and it felt like an interview room and not like the more sinister interrogation room—and sipping a cup of flavored coffee from the city's Keurig, he was starting to feel more curious than worried again. Keurigs have a bad reputation, he thought. Sure, there was no barista with an espresso machine and a steamer, but still, if the choices were varied (and they were in Frankenmuth), they were OK. He knew his thoughts were a little scattered by his day off going haywire. He wished he had a nice ceramic cup instead of Styrofoam, but he could see why they'd do that here. He sighed. Again, and again.

Finally, the chief arrived in the room with C.J. And they had some paperwork in front of them. The chief started out. "So how did you like the family reunion, Jim?" Jim thought that was an odd question.

"It seemed like a pretty bad reunion to me," he said. "Two people are dead, and that lawyer pissed everyone off enough that that one guy—Ned?—destroyed Lodge property. But otherwise, it was another couple shifts behind the bar for me. What's this about?"

Ed said, "Well, since you are part of the family, we were wondering how you wound up pouring drinks for them instead of enjoying the festivities with the rest of them."

Jim about spit out his caramel café au lait at that. "Have you lost your mind? That's not my family. I'm an employee of the Lodge serving up drinks like every week, a neutral and somewhat captive observer. I don't know any of those people, but now that you mention it, they do seem strange."

"Oh, I think you aren't being square with us, Jim," responded Ed, sliding the DNA report across the table to Jim.

Jim shoved it right back. "What is this? It looks like gobbledygook to me."

"This," said Ed dramatically, holding up the sheet of paper, "shows that you are the son of Virginia Stanley."

Jim, a bright enough guy who had taken in the reading of the will moment choreographed by Barney and the deceased Virginia while he garnished second rounds, now looked like he might faint.

45: SURPRISE!

"Obviously, the lab got the DNA mixed up," Jim said to Ed and C.J. "There's absolutely no way I'm related in any way to those nuts, let alone being the child of Virginia Stanley. My mother is alive and well and living on her farm out in Millington. Since others in the room that day were related to Mrs. Stanley, it stands to reason that this is just a mistake in the lab," Jim concluded with finality.

C.J. responded first. "Jim, we have no idea if you know this or not and are reserving judgment on that for now, but you were adopted by the Schmidts in Ohio at the convent run by the Sisters of Mercy, who took in unmarried teenage pregnant girls and found homes for their babies. That's where you started out in this world, and Mrs. Stanley was the teenage girl whose baby the Schmidts adopted."

"How can you possibly know that when I don't even know that, nor do I believe it."

"It's absolutely true," Ed interjected. "The nuns still have the records of who took Virginia Stanley's baby, and it was your parents, the Schmidts. Frankly, I'm amazed you are denying this to such a degree since you stand to inherit millions as the only beneficiary under her will. Which gives you a huge motive for killing her. Why wait around tending bar when you could be living it up on Mom's millions?"

"My dad died a few years ago. I came home to this area to help my mother and be close to her since she has kept the farm. When you look into my finances, you'll see that I'm OK financially. I took the bartender job that Judy offered me because I thought it would be fun, which, up to this moment, it has been. If I'm not charged with a crime here, I want to go home."

"Home to your efficiency in town or home to your adopted mother's farm?" asked Ed.

"Home to wherever I want since I haven't done anything wrong."

"OK," said Ed. "You can go. But we are in the middle of two homicide investigations and have uncovered that you have quite a good motive to kill Mrs. Stanley. We aren't positive about the connection with Mark the carriage driver at this point. But start asking yourself what will convince us to look in another direction and we'll talk again soon."

"This is some serious bullshit," sputtered a now angry Jim.

"Do you want a ride to your car?" asked C.J.

"I've really fallen down the rabbit hole with you people. My car is two blocks away over by my apartment. Thanks, but I don't want another ride from you guys. Ever."

He slammed the door on the way out, not nearly as intimidated as they might expect from having been pushed on being the subject in a murder investigation.

"What do you think?" asked C.J.

"I think we better keep looking," said Ed. "We'll follow through on this guy, especially as he's the only one with a strong motive, not to mention the coincidence of everyone meeting up in Frankenmuth. But I'm a little less convinced he's our man now than before we talked to him."

46: NO APOLOGIES NECESSARY

Jim left the police station and decided he had to talk to the one person who knew the truth ... his mother. She lived on the family farm about thirty minutes from Frankenmuth. The farm had been in the Schmidt family for four generations. Jim had retired from the military when his dad died to help his mother remain on the farm as long as possible because that was important to her. She was now eighty three, and still there.

The land itself was rented to farmers who grew crops on it. Jim wasn't crazy about his mom living on the farm, but she was doing OK. He had hired a local woman who came in every day to help out in a variety of ways with mostly housekeeping chores, and Jim picked up groceries.

Jim was thinking about his life with his parents as he drove toward the house. He had had a happy childhood. His parents were hardworking, and there were always farm chores to do. Jim was an only child. His parents had told him he was their late-in-life baby—a gift from God. The odds of the police having confused the DNA report seemed remote, and he thought back on the lack of extended relatives that he had never given much thought to.

What if his parents hadn't wanted anyone to let the truth slip for whatever reason? They were independent, private people. He could imagine that.

When he graduated from high school with excellent grades, he decided that he wanted to join the army. He was adamant that he wanted to serve his country. He enlisted and reported for duty the summer after he graduated. When he left, his mother gave him a religious medal, a St. Christopher medal to assure safe travels, as a talisman that he carried with him everywhere.

After Desert Storm, he was honorably discharged from the military and full of plans to go to college and begin a new career. His parents were happy to have him back safe. But then love happened. Jim met Alice when they were working at the same restaurant; he was working the bar, and she waited tables.

Jim postponed college until they could afford tuition. His marriage, though, fell apart. He was restless and disappointed, not too sure where he was headed, but always visited the farm several times a year.

The day after 9/11, Jim—like so many—reenlisted. After his dad died, he again left the army, opting to be closer to his mother and helping her out financially. Working at the Lodge gave him flexibility and proximity to the farm. The day he arrived home from the army again, he carefully put the medal in a box in his dresser.

Now he wondered about that medal. Earlier, the lawyer had said that the nuns at the convent had given each baby a medal. Did the medal his mom gave him to keep him safe come from the nuns? His parents believed in God but weren't steady churchgoers, so Jim didn't really have an affinity for steady church attendance either. But he hung onto that medal like his life depended on it and to this day, he wasn't sure it didn't—perhaps the old foxhole theory of religion.

Jim pulled up to the farmhouse, looking like it had for 150 years. It was home. He opened the door and called to his mom. "Mom, it's me."

Dolores was in the kitchen, having her nightly cup of tea. "Jim! It's late. Is everything OK?"

Jim leaned down and kissed her. "I need to run upstairs for just a minute. I'll be right down."

When he returned, he sat down opposite his mom at the table and put the medal between them. "Mom, tell me about this medal."

Dolores stared at her teacup. "It's just a medal that I hoped would keep you safe."

"Mom, I know that I'm adopted. My birth mother—I think that's the right expression—has left me money, a lot of money."

Dolores looked up, crying. "You are my son. I am your mother."

Jim touched her hand. "And that's true forever. But a young girl from Ohio gave birth to me in a convent for unwed mothers. The police have discovered this while looking into a murder case. Mom, this is the craziest, most dumbass family you've ever seen."

"Language, James."

"Mom, tell me the truth." It was hard for him to watch tears rolling down her cheeks, but they had to have this conversation now. "I can only be grateful for the life I've had, thanks to you and Dad. It changes nothing between us."

"Jim, your dad and I wanted kids, lots of kids, and after many years, we realized that wasn't God's plan for us. I couldn't let it go. I used to go to church every day to pray for a child. I met a nun there one day who asked if she could help me.

"As it turned out, she could. She told me about the convent in Ohio and helped us contact them. Your father was skeptical, but a month later we got a letter saying that our application for adoption was approved. We just had to wait until they had a baby for us. Every time the phone rang, our hearts skipped a beat.

"Finally, the call came. Our son—you, Jim—was ready to pick up. Just like that, just that fast. When we got to the convent, we waited in the vestibule fifteen minutes. A nun finally came out with papers for us to sign. We signed, and there you were, all red and scrunchy. Pinned to your blanket was the medal I gave you, and a rosary was tucked into the folds.

"The trip home was amazing. I rocked you, told you stories, sang silly songs. We decided you were ours. No one would know you'd been adopted. You were James Schmidt."

Jim was puzzled. "But why not tell me?"

"Why? Why would you need to know? You are our son." Dolores sounded a little defensive.

"Well, it's a done deal. However, I seem to also be the son of Virginia Stanley, who left me her fortune. And she was murdered. So first I have to be one hundred percent cleared of her murder."

Dolores was shocked. "My son is no murderer."

"Mom, wait until you meet my biological cousins. Batshit crazy."

"James, language! I am exhausted and will not apologize for not telling you this story earlier. But please know, you have always been a very loved son by both your parents."

"That is forever, Mom. I've always known that."

47: TIFF'S

Nelly and Nora, no strangers to enjoying a drink or two, as everyone in town knew by now, stopped in at Tiffany's Food and Spirits, a bar/restaurant popular with both locals and tourists. The big front porch was a feature in the summer. The fun bar was decorated with a tin ceiling and Tiffany hanging lamps. Rumor had it that there was an original lamp somewhere in the bar.

They eventually got seated and each ordered a slice of pizza and a bottle of wine. Adam wandered over and took an extra chair at their table, uninvited.

"What's the word, ladies? Anything new happening with the crime wave in Frankenmuth or your batty family?"

Both Nora and Nelly bristled a bit at the disparaging description of their family.

"Well, our family might be batty, but we heard from a couple members of the Residenz staff that the police picked up the bartender for some kind of interrogation, and why would they?"

"Yeah," said Adam. "Why would they indeed?"

"Well," said Nora, "they might if he's the long-lost relative that Aunt Gin was so anxious to give her money to out of sheer spite."

"How the hell would they even know that?" wondered Adam. And he added for effect, "Does this mean you've all been served drinks by a double murderer?'"

"You weren't there of course, but they took the DNA of everyone who was around that day, including anyone working the reunion, and that, my friend, included Jim the bartender."

If Adam had been drinking martinis he would have choked on the olive.

"How in the world could this guy have the foresight to arrange to be working at an event where long-lost relatives were hanging out? I mean, how?"

"Coincidence?" suggested the twins in unison, a quality Adam found beyond grating.

"Now you two are sounding batty."

"You never heard of 'small world' stories, Adam?" asked Nelly. "You read about them all the time. I've personally experienced them. You go away to get far from home for a nice vacation, stay at some exclusive resort on a small island in a strange ocean, and up pops your boss taking a nice getaway with his girlfriend instead of his wife, and you've just witnessed it. I had that very thing happen once and it ended up causing me to look for work."

"Why should you look for work, angel? You had perfect blackmail material. I hope you snapped a picture with that phone."

Nora and Nelly both looked at him like an annoying bug that had landed in the middle of their table and might bite.

Adam excused himself, citing early business meetings the next day, and left by the back door.

Nelly and Nora looked at one another in silent exchange. Speaking as one, they both said, "That guy's cheese is vile." A passing waitress did a double take at the strange comment, wondering what sort of code phrase that was these days.

●●●

Meanwhile out back, Adam pulled out a black leather riding jacket, gloves, and a dark helmet from the bike he had parked in Tiffany's lot. He reached in the saddlebags and exchanged his shoes for riding boots. He had a couple of locations to check and anticipated a busy day tomorrow. A well of rage swelled in him—not at the Cheese Haus snippy buyer, not at Virginia, whom he hadn't seen in decades, and not at the twins who thought they were too good for him because truth be told, he knew they were. The rage was for that Ohio lawyer—Barney Mead. Barney ruined everything. And Barney was going to be sorry. He rode off, looking nothing like the benign colonel of chicken fame.

48: A DAY OF REST ... UNTIL ...

Poppy and Mary Ellen had agreed to meet at the coffee house to play mah-jongg. Barney had dismissed them for the day. He was off to follow up on the Schmidt family connection. That left a free morning to catch up with friends and perhaps win a few cents. When playing at the coffee house, tables usually played for money. Everyone had their dedicated mah-jongg purse filled with quarters, the usual penalty for losing a hand.

The girls were joined by Mary C. and Cheryl. It would be fun, fast-moving games with those two good players. As they set up the walls, they caught up with one another's lives. Mary had just moved and was thoroughly enjoying her new condo. She was glad Mary Ellen had brought her mah-jongg set as hers was buried under the chaos of the move.

Mary Ellen and Poppy shared that they had been busy helping a friend by doing some investigating. No one was surprised as Poppy had been a private investigator for years. Cheryl did ask if it involved dogs, which made everyone laugh. Poppy started to give a brief rundown on the Stanley situation when the coffee house door banged open. "Good morning, all!" Maisie was waving and walking toward the counter to order. Behind her trailed Clare.

"Clare?" Mary Ellen caught Clare's attention and motioned her over.

"Clare, are you OK? Are you out?" Mary Ellen asked without waiting for a response. Both Mary C. and Cheryl were clearly intrigued by this line of questioning.

"Mary Ellen and Poppy, good to see you. Well, um," Clare looked uncomfortable talking in front of people she didn't know. Mary C. and Cheryl excused themselves and went downstairs to allow some degree of privacy. "I'm out on bail. I confessed to putting medication in Virginia's flask. It may have contributed to her death even though that was not my intention. I have to wear an ankle tracker." She lifted her pants to show them the monitor. "Maisie hired me to clean houses, letting all the homeowners know the story. They all gave their permission. This is the greatest community ever, so I'll be able to pay some bills and maybe show I am not a bad person. I owe Maisie so much." She had tears in her eyes as she finished.

Poppy leaned over to Mary Ellen and said, "Full disclosure. I've had Clare cleaning house for me twice now what with Barney staying there and being busy with this case. I just haven't mentioned it to anyone."

Mary Ellen stood up and hugged her. Poppy was about to stand up when her smart watch pinged. She half stood while tapping and scrolling. "Mary Ellen, we have to go. Clare, good luck. Cheryl, can you pack up the set and we'll pick it up later?"

Mary Ellen was puzzled as she followed Poppy to the back door of the coffee house. "What's up?"

"Barney is taking Babycakes on a road trip. I'd like to see where they are going and make sure Babycakes has her harness on."

"Poppy, we have the Find It thing on our phones. We know where they will be going. Text Barney about the harness."

Clare heard every word about Babycakes off on a car ride with Barney headed to Millington and could hardly breathe worrying about the dog not being properly cared for. She headed for her own car.

At that moment, a motorcycle roared out of the parking lot. It startled Poppy and Mary Ellen so much they jumped.

"You're right. Cheryl has picked up the tiles by now. Do you want to get takeout wedges from Tiff's?"

"Sounds good. I'll tell you what, this cleaning lady thing isn't going to last at my house. Clare is just so peculiar around Babycakes. And you know that dog. She likes everyone. But she disappears when Clare's around. For her part, Clare is constantly trying to find her to gush over her. Dogs have a great sense of the weird. And even if she's not weird, it's enough for me the dog doesn't like her."

Poppy and Mary Ellen walked into the back door of Tiffany's Food and Spirits. They walked up to the bar and ordered three wedges, two regulars, and one with ranch instead of blue cheese for Todd. As they waited, they spotted the twins sitting at a table across the room. Mary Ellen grabbed Poppy, and they walked over.

"Good to see you both. We were at the will ..."

One of the twins responded quickly. "We remember you. After all, we've seen a lot of you this week."

Poppy said, "It has been a tough week for your family. Are you leaving soon?"

At that moment, the server came up behind Poppy. "Did the gentleman leave? Should I cancel his order?"

Nelly/Nora nodded and looked up at Mary Ellen. "Our friend Adam Brown had joined us and was called away on business. We're just waiting on an OK from the chief of police to leave. We had nothing to do with any of the deaths, so our presence here is no longer needed. Thanks for all your help." With that the twins put two twenties on the table and left.

Mary Ellen and Poppy turned around and went back to the bar. Angela brought out three boxed wedges. She had written Todd's name on his. The girls paid and left out the back door.

A few minutes later, Mary Ellen walked into her kitchen and yelled, "I brought Tiff's." She knew Todd would appear quickly, hoping it was a sausage-and-cheese deep-dish pizza that was a Tiff's specialty. He was still happy with his wedge.

"So how was mah-jongg? Did you win?"

"We didn't even play. Poppy got a message from Barney and thought she should rush home. Since we have that app on our phones, we decided we didn't need to rush off."

Todd, with a mouthful of lettuce and crumbled bacon, asked, "Was Tiff's crowded?"

"We ran into the twins from the Stanley murder. They are about to leave town. I guess Ed thinks they aren't involved. They were having lunch with some guy, Adam Brown?"

Todd looked up. "The guy with the knives and cheese? Who you know from the Lodge? The olive-pitter-thingy guy. How do they know him? This salad is so good!"

Mary Ellen stopped chewing. "What does he look like? Did I meet him?"

"Actually, he looks like Colonel Sanders, sort of."

"I'm calling Poppy. He's been in town all week. We saw him near the Cheese Haus, and he knows the twins. It may be nothing, but it's worth telling Ed. I don't know what's going on with that guy—possibly absolutely nothing—but we need to look into it."

Poppy answered on the first ring. As she listened to Mary Ellen, she grabbed her bag and keys and headed for the car.

49: GIL THE CROSSING GUARD NOTICES BABYCAKES OUT FOR A DRIVE

Whatever else was going on in town—and that turned out to be a lot—Gil had the rest of the day to himself, having covered the early shift. He had just put his pointy stop sign and other standard crossing-guard equipment into his car for a little outing he had been looking forward to. This afternoon he was planning on heading out to the village of Tuscola, where they had a country store that served decent ice cream. As he was about to hang a left on Genesee, he spotted some guy in a late-model Chevy sedan going a bit above the speed limit. And who was riding shotgun? Gil was positive it was Babycakes.

Altogether it was one of those "just ain't right" moments.

Gil had Poppy's phone number in his contacts because he often saw a dog he knew she was likely looking for (especially Munchie). He was sure he should let her know he saw her dog go by just in case Babycakes was snatched.

Poppy answered right away. "Gil! Hi. I'm heading over to the police station. What's going on?"

"Are you going to the police station because your dog is missing?"

"No, I'm not looking for a missing dog right now."

"No, Poppy! Are you missing Babycakes? Because I saw her going by in a red Chevy sedan with some guy I didn't recognize, and with a Harley Davison driven by a guy in strange pants hot on their heels."

"What? Oh! My Babycakes is taking a car ride with a friend who's here working on a legal case, Barney Mead. She's OK with him."

Gil said, "Is Barney traveling with some odd guy on a Harley?"

Poppy thought about the twins saying that Adam left them just before the mah-jongg players saw a revved-up bike heading south on Main, exceeding the speed limit, and got a bad feeling.

"Well, no. Barney shouldn't be traveling with any other vehicle. It's possible he really isn't with that bike, don't you think?"

"What I think is it's possible only one of them thinks they're together," said Gil.

"Oh, boy. I know where they might be going—out to Millington to a farm there. That's where Barney and Babycakes are headed. But I'm going to report this right away to Ed because I think we're going to need a police presence at the Schmidt farm."

"OK, Poppy. I'm going to fall back and follow in case there's a change of direction or anything else weird. I wouldn't want your Babycakes or your friend running into unexpected trouble."

"Thanks, Gil. Much appreciated. Be careful. Someone's around who's a killer and we still aren't positive who. There seems to be more than one person in the running." Poppy rang off and by then had pulled into the city parking lot and headed into the police station.

Mary Ellen was already there.

They told Ed everything they could think might be connected. The cheese guy who looked like Colonel Sanders; Barney headed with Babycakes over to the Millington Farm to talk to the widow who lived there and might know where her son was; Barney being followed by someone on a bike who may or may not be the Cheese Man; and Gil Rosin bringing up the rear to make sure no one veered off in an unexpected direction. They were unaware of Clare pursuing Babycakes.

Ed quickly brought Mary Ellen and Poppy up to date. "The heir is the bartender, you two. We have the DNA to prove it. He honestly seemed as shocked as anyone could be and is likely already at the Millington farm talking to his mom about the fact he's adopted."

Meantime, C.J. walked into the room in a state of excitement with a fax in her hand. "Look at this," she pretty much shouted.

Poppy, Mary Ellen, and the chief all looked. "Whoa!" said Mary Ellen. "That's the cheese guy, Adam Brown, who's been sort of romancing the twins and always seems to be hanging around. He tried to peddle a subpar cheese product over at the Cheese Haus and got tossed out. Why do you have his picture?"

"We finally got the results of some record searches on Virginia Stanley, including any marriages in her past. And guess what?"

"She's got an ex-husband," said Poppy.

"More intriguing than that, Poppy. She's got a husband and it's the—as you put it—cheese guy."

Mary Ellen leaned over the photo and said, "Wow! I saw Virginia's wedding photos and even all these years later, I can see the resemblance."

"Oh no! He's got to be the person following Barney and Babycakes to Millington right now who Gil saw. We need to all get right out there with reinforcements."

Ed said to C.J., "Call the Tuscola County sheriff's office and have him meet us at the farm in force. Tell him it's in relation to a double homicide that everyone knows we have going on here."

Everyone headed to vehicles. There was now a veritable convoy of peculiar vehicles headed to Millington, with Babycakes in the lead contentedly looking out the passenger window and enjoying the view and the unexpected ride with her good friend, Barney. Babycakes somewhere in the lizard part of her brain was relieved not to be with that odd cleaning person who seemed obsessed with being her friend. She knew that it was more than just the annoying vacuum. Like Gil watching the Harley go by, Babycakes had the "something ain't right" feeling about Clare.

Right now, the only road heading to Millington had more traffic than Main Street during Bavarian Fest.

50: BARNEY AND JAMES

Barney had checked his watch to make sure school had started before he turned onto Genesee Street. At lunchtime, Barney had a clear road ahead. Babycakes was riding shotgun, tethered by her canine seat restraint. With a speed limit of twenty-five miles per hour, he was able to notice the crossing guard looking surprised as he drove by. This was going to be a tricky visit. Mrs. Schmidt was a widow who now lived alone. Barney thought Babycakes might be a good icebreaker. Hopefully, she was a dog person. On her leash with her harness on, Babycakes was extremely well behaved—adorable, and she knew it.

The trip from Frankenmuth to Millington was only about twenty minutes. It was a scenic drive past farms and rural homes. With few cars on the road, Barney could afford to enjoy the drive. He did notice a motorcycle behind him. There were a few opportunities to pass, but the driver didn't seem interested in that option. Google finally alerted him that his destination was on the right. Barney put on his turn signal as soon as he saw the Centennial Farm sign in front of a brown-brick farmhouse. He pulled in and the motorcycle cruised on by.

Nothing about the property spoke of a working farm. The barns and outbuildings were faded, and doors were closed. The farmhouse itself was in good repair but didn't look as though there were any updates in the last fifty years.

Barney hooked Babycakes's leash to her harness, let her hop out of the car, and walked her to the front door. Although there was a doorbell that he pressed, no ring ensued so he opened the screen door and knocked on the wooden front door. Almost immediately the door was opened by an elderly woman, apparently annoyed.

"My goodness, I heard the bell. Just give me a second." Dolores wasn't excited to see a stranger standing on her porch. "Who are you?"

"Barney Mead, attorney at law, and this is my friend, Babycakes Lutz." Barney smiled, hoping Mrs. Schmidt might be attracted to the little dog.

"Mom, who's at the door?" said a voice from inside the house.

"A lawyer and a dog," said Dolores.

Jim came around the corner looking puzzled and put his arms around his mom's shoulders. Barney and Jim recognized each other at the same time. Barney looked startled as Jim held out his hand. "Nice to see you again, Sir. Mom, this is Mrs. Stanley's attorney. Please come in, Mr. Mead."

As Barney walked in, a motorcycle was passing the house slowly. Barney turned around to look at it. Something about that bike was making him uncomfortable.

Mrs. Schmidt led Barney and Babycakes into the living room. It was homey, with wooden floors and a braided rug, and a mixture of old and new furniture. On top of an old oak buffet was a fifty-five-inch TV. A well-used leather recliner had an old school desk as a side table. All the wood gleamed with polish.

"Would you like coffee? Should I get the dog some water?"

"That would be great, Mrs. Schmidt, then we can sit down and talk."

A loud noise on the front porch startled everyone. Jim got up to see what was going on, but before he got to the foyer, the door flew open.

51: FULL HOUSE

While Dolores remained in the kitchen preparing drinks and looking for a bowl that she was OK with Babycakes using, Adam Brown—known throughout most of the town as the Cheese Man or "that guy who looks like Col. Sanders"—charged his way into the house. He would look amusingly ridiculous in his khaki cargo pants and leather motorcycle boots and jacket if he weren't also waving a gun. There were surprises all around.

Adam yelled, "Everyone stay where you are."

Barney said, "You might want to put that gun down and leave before it goes off, and you spend the rest of your life in a Michigan prison."

Jim yelled, "Get out of my mother's house now!"

Adam yelled, "I'm the one with the gun!"

●●●

Dolores heard all this from the kitchen and reached behind her, pulling out the double aught which always sat in the corner to scare away varmints. It was often loaded and rarely ever used, but it didn't require a lot of skill to point.

Suddenly she spotted two women looking through the kitchen window at her. "What now?" she thought. But she went over to the kitchen entrance while raised voices continued arguing from the other room. She let Mary Ellen and Poppy in. She signaled them to keep quiet and Poppy whispered that the police were right behind them.

Dolores indicated that the invader had a gun.

Mary Ellen took the shotgun from Dolores, who was glad to relinquish it to someone else.

•••

"You!" Adam yelled at Barney. "You're the whole reason I'm here. You've completely screwed up my life and my plans, and I'm here to make you pay for that."

"Slow down here," said Barney. "Who are you? Why would you think I screwed up your life? I don't even know you."

"I'm Virginia's husband. All her money should have been mine now that she's dead. But you had to come up with a kid!"

"Oh my God. You killed my client—you killed Virginia?"

•••

Adam thought to himself that he just never came out on top, no matter how well he planned things. Success was always snatched from him. He should kill—he had to kill—everyone in this house. He'd already put up with every possible insult in this snooty little town, and some lawyer named "Barney" showed up and redirected all the money to some "kid" he never knew existed. Adam was beyond crazed over this. He also expected there might be an old lady here, but he wasn't worried about that. He could kill her last.

•••

Adam screamed, "Hey, I'm the one with the gun! Everyone take a seat while I sort this out, and keep your hands where I can see them."

Clare charged into the house at this point and found herself in the kitchen with Poppy, Mary Ellen, and Dolores, with Mary Ellen holding the shotgun. Everyone was so shocked to see Clare—especially Dolores, who had no idea who she was—that Mary Ellen loosened her grip on the shotgun. Clare, sensing opportunity, reached over and grabbed it from her. The house was so noisy no one was really aware of what was happening from one room to the next.

Poppy, trying to keep her voice low, said to Clare, "Why are you here, Clare? And why are you holding the shotgun?"

Clare responded, "I've come to take Babycakes out of her dangerous situation and have her come live with me where she belongs, with someone who truly loves her and wants to give her a good home. She wants to be with me."

Poppy was dumbfounded. "Don't be an ass, Clare! She's my dog, and she's fine."

"If she's so fine, why is she barking?"

Indeed, in the other room, Babycakes was barking up a storm right in Adam's face. He kicked her with one of his motorcycle boots and connected solidly with Babycakes's ribs, sending her squealing toward Barney. Poppy reacted to the sound by charging into the room with all the hostages. Babycakes was crawling in her direction. Clare screamed, "I'm coming, Babycakes!" as Mary Ellen retook possession of the shotgun.

Just as it appeared that someone was surely going to get shot by Adam or hurt one way or another by Clare, both of whom were flummoxed at all these people and ready to panic, Mary Ellen walked in and racked the shotgun. That caught everyone's attention. Barney and Jim weren't quite relieved yet, but they were both glad to see her.

Dolores remained in the kitchen per Poppy's instruction, hoping to keep Clare under some kind of control. She had some confidence that so many people ought to be able to stop this guy. But she didn't want her son or that dog harmed. Even the lawyer seemed nice enough for a lawyer. She had no clue who any of the women were, but certainly the one in the kitchen with her was deranged. How had her life changed so drastically in a couple of minutes?

Adam, shaking from adrenaline and panic that everything was out of control, didn't see a reinvigorated and very out-of-sorts Babycakes coming at him. She managed a jump that allowed her to hang on, like the small bulldog she was, to Adam's right thigh, remarkably high for such a short dog. Jim and Barney both winced. "Oh my God! Stop! Stop! Owwwww," Adam screamed, dropping the pistol.

Jim finally was able to do something useful, to his relief, and grabbed the dropped gun.

Just as the three men—Adam, Jim, and Barney—figured this had played out and ought to be resolved until the police arrived, Gil, the ex-cop crossing guard, came running through the kitchen with his octagonal stop sign full of jagged points and clobbered Adam on the side of the head with it.

"Where did you come from?" asked Barney.

"We'll talk later," said Gil.

Poppy wasn't sure where Gil had come from, but she knew from his phone call that he was in the vicinity and the stop sign was perfect. She, still blindly angry over the assault on Babycakes, started kicking Adam over and over in his ribs with her sneakers. The chaotic moment only felt more chaotic with Babycakes frantically barking and snarling while all this was going on. People were beginning to feel sorry for Adam. Clare emerged with a makeshift leash from somewhere and looped it around Babycakes's head, starting to drag the offended and furious Boston terrier toward the door.

Mary Ellen, thinking the shotgun was overkill at this point, picked up Gil's stop sign and clocked Clare on the back of the head with it. Clare went down, loosening her grip on the panicked dog.

Jim leaped forward to pull Poppy off Adam, which worked for a moment, only to find that his mother jumped in with one more sound kick to Adam's ribs. "Mom!" he shouted. "We've got him now! You might pull something kicking this guy. Please stop! And why is the caterer here?" Jim asked no one in particular, looking at Clare sitting on the floor, rubbing the back of her head.

At that, Poppy, still outraged but in control, shocked everyone, including her investigative partner Mary Ellen, by deftly flipping Adam over and handcuffing him. Her wig might just be slightly askew, she thought, but the threat had been neutralized. Mary Ellen now had the shotgun aimed at Clare just for emphasis, which gave Poppy some comfort that whatever weirdness was going on with Clare was under control.

Mary Ellen, speaking to the handcuffed Adam, said, "We can see why you killed Virginia—obviously for her money, so don't deny that—but why did you kill Mark?"

Adam responded, "He knew too much and was going to put it together. He didn't have to die, but he got scared and greedy, and grabbed for the knife. I had no choice."

"So why are we here?"

Adam tried to shout but the pressure of the handcuffs kept his voice at a low register. "To kill that lawyer who caused me to lose my inheritance."

Barney reacted. "Were you expecting to be in her will? You're really an idiot. She had a codicil that specifically cut you out in the event you were still alive. No one else got to hear that part since chaos broke out. But you, my friend, were never ever in the picture and now you're going to prison."

Everyone breathed a sigh of relief for a quick second. And a second was about all it took for a SWAT team to be the newest people to crash through the front door to save the hostages.

C.J. and Ed looked with some amazement at a scene with a lot more people than they expected to find, and what was more, the killer neutralized and under control. If he really was the killer. Because there was the caterer again—yet again!— thought Ed. She looked dazed and was being held at the point of a shotgun by Mary Ellen. Ed had to admit to himself that despite all odds, Mary Ellen still looked color coordinated and with her hair unmussed. Poppy looked like she'd been in a fight.

Ed's first comment was, "You've got handcuffs, Poppy?"

Mary Ellen chimed in, "I didn't know that either. Shouldn't we both have some? We need to talk about our budget for these things."

C.J.'s first comment, after Ed collected all the weapons on the scene, was to Adam. "You're under arrest for murder, kidnapping, assault, breaking and entering, and whatever else we figure out."

Poppy shouted, "And animal cruelty."

"Animal cruelty?" questioned C.J. "OK. Animal cruelty." She went on to Mirandize him.

Ed took it from there, turning to Clare. "You are under arrest on suspicion of … a lot of things … but let's say breaking and entering for starters, maybe conspiracy to commit murder, and we'll figure it all out at the jail." And she was Mirandized.

The Tuscola County sheriff talked to Ed and decided to escort the Frankenmuth police back to the station with the prisoner and facilitate getting him to the Saginaw County jail. The woman referred to as Clare the Caterer they'd leave in Frankenmuth for Ed to figure out. Again. Adam, though, had indeed killed two people in a town where no one killed anyone. No point taking chances with him now.

The Tuscola deputy sheriffs all knew Gil back in his working days as a fellow cop and offered him a ride back to town. They had spotted his car with a flat tire on the side of the road almost a mile away. That answered the question of his oddly timed arrival. But the irony of clobbering a killer with a sign that said STOP wasn't a bad reaction, they all decided. Once a cop….

•••

The old saying, "it takes a village," could mean a lot of things, depending on circumstances, thought Ed. He looked around the room and felt that everyone played a pretty good role in this, although he would have liked to have made it to the scene before Poppy and Mary Ellen. You couldn't have the local dog dick beating the cops to a double murderer.

He still wasn't positive if Poppy actually brought Babycakes to the farm with her, although he couldn't imagine how else she got there. He thought, if she's going to use a dog as part of her private investigator tools, she could stand to get one that looked a little more threatening. He also thought the normally cheerful Babycakes looked … what? … out of sorts? And she had a chunk of some khaki-colored cloth hanging off her lower teeth and had a low motor of a growl aimed at Clare. He supposed they'd get to the bottom of all the little mysteries he noticed in the room soon enough. The house was very crowded but remarkably undamaged.

Barney was happy enough a killer had been caught with no more loss of life, but sorry he had pulled Babycakes into it, thus upsetting his old friend. He was thinking David might not have been pleased with that move, Babycakes being an innocent, as David would have said. But he had found his heir, one who wasn't going to jail, and Frankenmuth's killing spree was over. And later it would sort out that Clare would need to do some considerable court-ordered time with mental health professionals. It appeared that Adam and Clare were unacquainted.

C.J., breaking her always professional demeanor, high-fived every woman in the room on her way out the door and nodded to the men.

Ed reminded Poppy and Mary Ellen to stop by the police station and give a full statement right away while everything was fresh in their heads. Meantime, Ed and one of his uniformed officers sat down to take Dolores's statement on the spot, along with Barney's and Jim's. By the time they got through with those, they were indeed convinced that they had solved a double homicide at last—what they hoped would be the only incident of its kind in Frankenmuth. And they had also stopped a rogue caterer while they were at it.

Ed called Judy because he knew how upsetting it was to have her own property involved in a murder. He could hear her beaming at the other end of the line. "Great job, Ed. I'm so glad to hear this news. Did those local investigators, Mary Ellen and Poppy, help out?"

After a moment's hesitation, Ed cryptically replied, "Those girls didn't get in our way." Judy gave a little eye roll that she knew was safe on the phone and said, "Good deal."

For their part, Mary Ellen and Poppy knew that Barney was good for every billable hour and they had racked up quite a few. They knew they didn't solve all this singlehandedly, but they were happy that they helped quite a bit, especially when it came to finding Virginia's missing heir, so they felt pretty professional about the whole thing.

They both stopped by the station, Babycakes in tow, before heading home, knowing that fresh information was more likely accurate information. Poppy might not have mentioned exactly how many times she kicked the Cheese Man. She hadn't counted. And apparently no one else had either.

It was a wrap.

52: NEWS AT 6:00, REDUX

Mary Ellen sat on the couch with Todd, each with a glass of wine. It had taken Todd a bit to simmer down after Mary Ellen decided it was better if he heard about the farm visit and the shotgun from her instead of rumors around town, which were inevitable. For her part, Mary Ellen was happy to be home, pleased that the case was successfully over, and definitely ready for a cuddle with her man. Nothing on the news was a big surprise to her, of course. Todd blanched at some of the more detailed description of violence—both real and avoided—involved in the capture of the killer. He thought he would never pit another olive. He glanced at Mary Ellen when it was implied by the newscaster that a private detective had subdued the killer. She reassured him it wasn't her. He rolled his eyes and muttered under his breath, "Poppy. Naturally."

Barney had packed up and left town as soon as his interview with the police was over. He had clients backed up from spending longer than expected there. It was great to see Poppy again, and he was sorry David was gone. He wondered if he needed a dog, but reality gripped him. Not while he was still in the midst of those seven-day working weeks, easily twelve hours a day a lot of the time, and complete absorption in whatever task was at hand. Nonetheless, Barney turned on the news at six o'clock because it was all over the state this time. He noticed he as well as his surprisingly effective investigators, Poppy and Mary Ellen, weren't mentioned by name. He smiled at that. Utterly predictable.

The last two remaining nuns at Sisters of Mercy were also tuned into the news. As unflappable as they were, they found the whole story amazing. A few weeks later, a generous check landed on their desk. It didn't change a thing.

Poppy had popcorn and her Babycakes on her lap, watching the news report. She had made the popcorn earlier and offered some to Tim and Sue next door. It was an excuse to see what the heck was going on in their hot tub. They were such helpful, quiet neighbors, but she suspected they had a secret wild life revolving around that fancy tub. Some things you don't investigate, she thought. But she kept an ear open. She felt a vague premonition about that tub.

She laughed out loud at the omission of her and Mary Ellen's names. Everyone that mattered knew. She laughed again, thinking of the running joke among her friends about fixing her up with a man. They knew as well as she did that she was married forever. She stroked Babycakes's tall ears that heard every sound, and they were both content. As if to punctuate that idea, Babycakes gave a big snuffle of satisfaction at being home, just the two of them now that company had moved on.

Father Bob sat in a clubhouse after a late-afternoon round of golf in South Carolina—even there, he could see the news. He shook his head with a hint of a smile and had another drink with the other Tim and Sue in town (like the Sharons, names overlapped in Frankenmuth) as well as Gary and Ethel. Retirement wasn't so bad, he decided. And neither was lending a hand on the periphery of an investigation. All five of the Frankenmuthers were amazed at a double homicide in town.

Judy wouldn't have missed that news report. She watched to the end, said, "Ha!" and went back to work. She wrote a reminder note to give her Cheese Haus manager a bonus for not buying any cheese from a killer and made a mental reminder to talk her mom out of personal book signings, thinking of the strange dude she herself very nearly bought an olive pitter from. Signings after you're one hundred, she thought, weren't necessary.

And in the List home, Rick shouted to Karen, "Have you seen Munchie?" Karen reached down, patted the big black-and-white head, and said, "He's right by my side."

EPILOGUE

Mary Ellen gave Todd a quick kiss. "I'm going to meet Poppy at the Kaffee Haus. I'll be back for lunch."

"Be careful, we got about two inches of snow, which I've cleared off the driveway, and it's going to pick up after noon."

Frankenmuth in the weeks after Christmas was calm. Most people had taken down their big, outside decorations. Mary Ellen and Todd had hauled in Santa, who stood guard at the corner of their house. Many houses still left lights up for Snowfest, which was at the end of January. Poppy kept seasonal lights up inside just to mitigate the short days as well as her snowman collection, which lasted almost until spring.

She was already at the Kaffee Haus, seated in one of the chairs facing the wall-hung fire installation. It was a cozy place for a chilly January morning.

"How are you?" Poppy greeted Mary Ellen. "I'm glad to finally see you in person rather than on text messages." The friends had texted each other a lot, but because of family visitors and weather, they had really not had time to catch up. Friends had already started leaving for points south. Winter for residents who stayed was an entirely different experience in Frankenmuth.

"True! It's been a while." Mary Ellen started to unwrap all of her winter gear. "It is brutal out there."

"So, we both had to switch dentists after you tracked down that affair with the hygienist. I haven't been to see the new one since then. Have you?"

"Yes. He's fine. We just have to drive out of town now. Maybe we should change our cards to include 'Lost Dogs; Unfaithful spouses; Frankenmuth murders.'"

Poppy laughed as she looked at her friend. "Still covered in dog hair, I see." Mary Ellen had had her children's two golden retrievers, Granby and Finnegan, visit. Poppy had had the job of chasing them both, and of course, returning them both. Mary Ellen smiled as she tried, to little effect, to brush off her black pants. As their cappuccinos arrived, they both settled in for a long chat.

"I had an interesting talk with Father Bob last week. An anonymous contribution arrived at the Sisters of Mercy. It was a very generous amount. He asked if I knew anything about it. I told him I suspected it came from someone who was grateful for their services. 'They'll put it to good use,' he said."

Poppy and Mary Ellen were sure they would.

Mary Ellen said, "So I sent a Christmas card to the Stanleys—each individual family, I mean." Mary Ellen sent a lot of Christmas cards, so Poppy wasn't surprised. "I actually heard back from the twins. As it turned out, Virginia had put the family mansion in all four of the cousins' names. On her death, they each owned one-fourth of the property. The twins bought out Joe and Ned's portion and have moved in. The house is both their business and their home. Ned and Joe have been able to use the money to fund their future endeavors, however that goes for them. They get the chance, anyway, to pursue those dreams."

"We had a very interesting fall. Did you get your check from Barney?" Poppy asked. "It's so much fun getting paid for more than the usual dog retrievals. I bought a heat lamp for the deck. We were able to have s'mores using the fire table on Christmas Eve. Babycakes and the grandkids thought that was pretty special."

"Maybe we can get back to the mah-jongg table more often now," said Mary Ellen. "Do you have any time to play next week?"

Poppy sighed, "That would be great. Who with?"

"We've got a table. You, me, Louise, and Bootsie."

"Man. It takes all day to play three games with Bootsie. I don't know if I can do it."

"Oh, come on, Poppy. So many people are in Florida. Let's play with Bootsie."

Poppy's smart watch dinged. "Oh, good grief. Speak of the devil, and I don't mean Bootsie. Barney's wondering if he can come for a long weekend. He really loved Frankenmuth. Hotels, of course, are booked."

Barney, Poppy, Mary Ellen, and Babycakes together again? Mary Ellen smiled, and Poppy raised an eyebrow. You never knew what would happen in Frankenmuth, as it turned out.

Acknowledgments

Thanks to the many people who made this book possible and helped in the creative and publishing process so expertly.

Specifically, we would like to acknowledge Judy Zehnder Keller, whose giant presence in the city of Frankenmuth made her an ideal person to share ideas with and take suggestions from. She was always right, and she is missed.

We are grateful for the generous support of the Bavarian Inn Lodge.

To our Friends and friends at the Frankenmuth Wickson District Library, thank you for all your support. Thanks also go to Joan Ramm and Taylor Lutz for their early reading of the original manuscript and spot-on suggestions.

Thanks to our illustrator, Lane Trabalka, who went from fourteen to sixteen years old in the process of our writing this book. Her artistic talent with all the illustrations adds an element of creativity beyond words.

Thanks to a considerable number of friends, from Frankenmuth and beyond town, who were encouraging and even pleased to see a little of themselves portrayed in the book. They have been behind us every step and have shared great ideas. What can be more priceless than friends?

Thank you to our project manager, Tanya Muzumdar, and her team from Mission Point Press for their expertise, guidance, red pencil, and encouragement. It made for a great deal of conversation and a better book.

Thanks to the dedicated people at Midwest Boston Terrier Rescue for the real life Babycakes and for saving the lives of thousands of fabulous dogs under almost always difficult circumstances.

From Roz: Thanks to my son and daughter-in-law, James and Gladys Crawford, who make a near impossible journey every year with the world's most loving grandkids—Miguel, Zane, and Tyckoski. And thanks to my kind-spirited daughter, Crissy, who always has a surprise or two.

From Susan: Thanks to my daughter, gretchen, and my son, Jason, and daughter-in-law, Sheehan, for their interest, suggestions, and support. And to my wonderful husband, Mel—I owe you a cigar.

ABOUT THE AUTHORS AND ILLUSTRATOR

ROZ WEEDMAN

Roz Weedman lives in the tourist town of Frankenmuth, Michigan. She worked for thirteen years as a legal secretary, continued her education at the University of Michigan, and eventually retired from her position as a professor of English after twenty years. Her teaching career focused on writing and American literature. For pleasure, she reads mysteries from Louise Penny, Anthony Horowitz, Ian Rankin, Agatha Christie, and other masters of the genre. Roz loves nothing more than playing mah-jongg with her friends and grandkids. She believes road trips are the best trips. If you're in Frankenmuth, she's easy to find. Her white minivan with the Mahj license plate will be parked askew somewhere in town.

COOKIE WEEDMAN

Cookie Weedman, rescued during the pandemic by Midwest Boston Terrier Rescue, and the inspiration for Babycakes.

Susan Todd

Susan Todd lives in Frankenmuth, Michigan, with Mel, her husband of over fifty years. After being a stay-at-home mom, she went back to get her teaching degree. She started her work at the same college her son was attending. After graduating, Susan and Mel moved to Frankenmuth, where she taught elementary and middle school for eleven years. Since retiring they enjoy traveling both abroad and in the US. They have a daughter, gretchen, and a son, Jason. If you travel to Frankenmuth and see a silver-blue convertible zipping around town, give Susan a wave.

Lane Trabalka, illustrator

Lane Trabalka is a visual arts 2D concentration student in tenth grade at an arts and sciences school in Saginaw. She enjoys noticing, mulling over, and sometimes drawing the finer details of the world around her.